DREAM ENDER

THE BAILEY SPADE SERIES: BOOK 4

DIMA ZALES

♠ MOZAIKA PUBLICATIONS ♠

Published by Mozaika Publications, an imprint of Mozaika LLC.
www.mozaikallc.com

Cover by Orina Kafe
www.orinakafe.design

e-ISBN: 978-1-63142-617-9
Print ISBN: 978-1-63142-618-6

CHAPTER ONE

I'M KISSING VALERIAN.

This is my second time kissing in the real world, and it's glorious. The hospital room around me spins on its axis. My fingers are buried in his thick, silky hair, and his lips are soft and smooth, his tongue skillfully—

Someone rudely clears his throat.

I stiffen. Before that moment, the thought of bacteria and viruses couldn't have been further from my mind, but now, images of post-nasal drip invade my consciousness, ruining the mood.

Valerian draws back from me and glares at the intruder—a bashful-looking Felix, who looks extra thin without his robot suit.

"I'm sorry." Felix backs out of the room. "I—that is, the others… If you're up, we should head back."

Head back. To Gomorrah. Right.

As much as I hate to have been interrupted from

what Valerian and I were doing, going back is an excellent idea. Between the boost to my dreamwalker powers and the revelation about my not-so-dead twin, getting to Mom is at the top of my priority list.

"We're on a post-apocalyptic world ravaged by a deadly virus," Felix says, still sounding defensive. "It's not exactly a place to Netflix and chill."

Valerian must show Felix something with his powers because he pales, turns on his heel, and sprints away.

"We should go," I say reluctantly, my eyes on Valerian's sensuous lips.

"To be continued," he murmurs into my ear and strides out of the room.

With a sigh, I follow.

When I was brought to this hospital from Necronia, I was barely conscious. Now that I'm walking through the white corridors with my awareness intact, I wish someone would knock me out again so I wouldn't see all the dead bodies sprawled around.

The virus Icelus had planned to unleash on Necronia had made its way here first, with deadly results.

The dreariness follows me all the way outside, where our team is waiting inside a circle of corpses that are standing upright. That's thanks to Rowan, the necromancer who left Necronia with us.

As we approach, she pushes her signature steampunk-style goggles higher up on her head to combat a few unruly strands of her strangely colored hair—half of her head is bleached white, the other half is jet black. Behind her is Fabian in his musclebound man form, dressed for once. Next to him is Dylan, her long brown hair uncharacteristically disheveled and her blank eyes lacking the razor-sharp intelligence that always made them so lively. Itzel, our gnome friend, and Ariel, Felix's uber roommate, are with them also.

Spotting me, Ariel flashes a radiant smile that shows off her uber-perfect teeth.

"Finally. Sleeping Beauty awakens," Rowan says to me. "I bet there was a kiss involved." She winks at Valerian.

Felix reddens and Valerian shakes his head, while Itzel just huffs into her breathing mask.

"Newly made zombies?" I ask Rowan, glancing at the upright corpses.

She nods. "I gathered some *helpers* for our trip." She emphasizes the preferred Necronian term.

Ariel looks worriedly down the street. "It's a good thing she did. The Overtaken attacked us twice while you were out."

I scan the zombie herd, but of course, in death, the Overtaken look identical to other corpses. "Twice? I didn't realize there were enough people left alive on this world to Overtake."

"There are," Felix says. "In fact, while you were out, I was able to locate a computer in the hospital and use my powers to get into this world's equivalent of the internet. I spread the formula for the cure as widely as I could. Should give the survivors a chance."

Ariel smacks Felix approvingly on the shoulder. "I wonder if the Councils could leave some ready-made cure here when they bring it to Necronia."

"I'll tell them to do so," Valerian says. "Now we should head out before more Overtaken attack. We have no cure for *that* problem."

Fabian pushes the zombies aside and hands me and Valerian our Gomorran guns. Once we have those stashed, he also gives me my katana and Valerian his sai.

Dylan is still standing there, her gaze unfocused.

"Dylan," I say formally. "I wanted to thank you. If you hadn't come through with the cure, Valerian and I would be part of Rowan's zombie herd."

At the mention of her name, Dylan looks in my general direction but doesn't meet my gaze. Nor does she acknowledge the thanks.

Weird.

She hadn't acted like this before.

Is this one of the side effects of Rowan bringing her from the dead? With a pang of guilt, I recall Rowan saying Dylan wouldn't be the same, yet Valerian, Fabian, and I pressured her to perform the special resurrection anyway.

Then something else catches my attention. With the exception of Itzel, no one is wearing masks anymore—despite the fact that we're on a virus-infected world.

When I ask about it, Dylan seems to perk up a little. "The cure isn't just a cure," she says with a hint of her usual professorial tone. "It works prophylactically as well."

Ah, so they all drank it. Smart.

Rowan runs a hand through the bleached side of her hair. "Let's go."

She and Fabian cross the street, with zombies and the rest of us close behind.

We enter the train station again, and thanks to Rowan, the purplish corpses lying around join our herd of zombies.

Due to sheer numbers, our procession takes a while to navigate the maze of corridors into the hub, where I watch Rowan do something strange: She grabs the nearest zombie by the hand, that zombie grabs the hand of another, and so on. They daisy-chain like that until everyone is holding hands, like a bunch of macabre kindergarteners.

"It's the only way I can get them through the gate," Rowan explains. "This way, they register as my possessions."

I dart a guilty glance at Dylan.

Rowan bends over and places Frank, her resurrected opossum-like pet, in a sack hanging crosswise over her body. "Dylan is still Cognizant. I think she'll be able to get through without me. Hopefully."

Fabian extends his hand to Dylan. "How about we don't take any chances."

If I were Dylan, I'd make sure to point out that I'm

not Fabian's possession, but she just meekly grabs his hand while avoiding the werewolf's eyes.

Puck. I really hope this odd behavior is temporary.

Valerian looks at Rowan. "Where's the body of your betrothed?"

"We questioned him while you were out," she says. "Keyser didn't know much. The ancient vampire had glamoured him to thwart anyone who mentions the word 'Icelus.' That was also when he'd gotten infected and was told about the nightmare that made him into an Overtaken."

"What about all the vampires we killed on Necronia?" Valerian asks. "Could you bring them back for questioning?"

"I tried," Rowan says. "I guess it doesn't work with dead vampires—which kind of makes sense, seeing how it's their second death and all."

Valerian curses under his breath. "We desperately need intelligence on our enemy."

I put a hand on his shoulder. "Maybe Maxwell will have something for us when we get to Gomorrah." I look at Dylan. "Did he tell you anything on that topic in your dreams?"

Dylan doesn't respond.

"Dylan," Fabian says soothingly. "Did you sleep?"

She shakes her head.

Rowan pats the sack where she's stashed her pet. "Frank doesn't sleep either."

Neither do vampires—another type of the undead—but it wouldn't be courteous to mention that.

"Let's go," Rowan says, and before anyone can object, she leads her zombie train into the pink plasma gate.

We step out on a hub located in a lush forest meadow where we'd camped on the way to Necronia.

"This time, let everyone else go first," Valerian says to Rowan as we approach the next gate. "That way, if there's an attack, we can cover your arrival."

With a barely perceptible eye roll, Rowan gestures for everyone to go ahead, like a doorman.

Ariel, Fabian, and Dylan take the lead, Itzel and Felix step in next, and Valerian goes right before me.

When I come out on the other side, it's to the sound of battle.

CHAPTER TWO

FRANTICALLY, I take in the situation.

There are about a hundred enemies swarming the hub, all in various sleepwear. Their fiery eyes make it clear why they're trying to kill us.

They're the Overtaken.

Great. Just great. All I want is to get to Mom and try to wake her up, but pucking Phobetor isn't going to make it easy, is he?

Whipping out my gun, I hold it so tightly my knuckles whiten.

Time to fight.

But first, I flip my gun to the nonlethal setting. The Overtaken aren't bad people; they're being used by one. Or more specifically, by a bad god of nightmares.

A woman in her nightie hurls a skillet at my head.

I duck, and the lead projectile whizzes by my ear.

Without taking time to aim, I shoot my attacker in the chest.

She collapses.

A burly man rushes at me, arms outstretched. I take a fighting stance, but before I can so much as block a hit, Valerian puts my attacker down with his gun.

Fabian is now in his wolf form. Swinging his massive paw, he smashes it in the face of one of the attackers, breaking the woman's skull into pieces.

Puck. So much for sparing lives.

One of the Overtaken stops attacking and looks straight at me and Valerian. "I wanted the two of you to suffer from the virus," he snarls. He doesn't feel that way, of course; it's Phobetor speaking through his mouth. "Since you're so stubborn, I'll have to dispatch you like this, with violence."

"You can try," Valerian grits out and shoots the speaker.

The guy drops.

"Resistance is futile," Phobetor says through the mouth of a large man and has him lunge at Itzel.

Puck.

I aim at him but miss.

Backing away, Itzel launches a lightning ball at her attacker. He flies back and lands on his back.

Yes! We might just get out of this yet.

"Did the god of nightmares just quote the Borg?" Felix asks, panting. "Does that mean he's seen *Star Trek*?"

Phobetor must not like it when mortals criticize the authenticity of his villainous quips or his taste in TV shows. A thin woman leaps at Felix with a meat tenderizer.

Puck. Without his robot suit, he might not be able to take her on.

She swings the tenderizer at his head.

Felix sidesteps, but just barely.

Heart pounding, I aim and shoot.

The woman drops to the ground.

Ariel knocks out the Overtaken next to her, then casts an exasperated glance at Felix. "*Star Trek?* Seriously?"

Felix shrugs and dodges a colander flying at his head while I shoot the person who threw it.

Behind me, Rowan appears with her daisy chain of zombies.

Finally, some reinforcements.

Problem is, the zombies are still clearing the gate, and I don't think Rowan can let go of their hands, else she'll lose most of them.

For now, we're still on our own.

Phobetor must see the writing on the wall because the Overtaken attack with renewed vigor. My teammates retaliate. Ariel knocks a woman out with a blow to the temple, while Fabian breaks a few arms and legs. Through all this, Dylan is staying back; she appears to still be coming to terms with the shock of her second chance at life.

Rowan's last zombie clears the gate, and she has them unlock hands and leap at the Overtaken.

I shoot a few of our enemies to help, but it's no

longer necessary. Within seconds, the Overtaken are on the ground, held down by zombie hands.

Wiping the sweat off my forehead with my sleeve, I lower my gun and turn to Dylan. "We should give these Overtaken the cure for the virus. Our zombies might be contaminated."

Dylan's face doesn't change in any way to indicate that she's heard me. However, she takes out an ampule and proceeds to pour the liquid down the throats of Phobetor's victims.

After the cure has been distributed, Valerian walks around and methodically knocks them all out with his gun.

Meanwhile, Dylan trudges over to the body of the Overtaken whose skull Fabian crushed. Once there, she kneels, as if in mourning.

Felix cocks his head. "Has her resurrection made her more compassionate?"

Rowan sucks in a breath. "I hope it's not what I think."

We rush over to where Dylan is kneeling, and just as slurping sounds reach my ears, I realize this must be what Rowan was hoping against.

Dylan isn't mourning the woman.

She's eating her brain.

CHAPTER THREE

I FIGHT A GAGGING SENSATION. So, so gross. "Brains can contain infectious prions," I say out loud. "Think mad cow disease and the like. Eating is how you get them into your body."

Felix tears his gaze away from Dylan. "Is that the only reason not to eat them?"

"Well, no." I shudder. "I'd rather starve to death."

Fabian turns back into a person and looms over Rowan in all his naked glory. "What's happening?"

Rowan steps back. "I didn't want to bring her back, remember? Sometimes taboos exist for good reasons. I told you there would be side effects."

"That's not a side effect," Fabian growls. "That's a full-blown effect."

Rowan glances at the sack where she's keeping her pet. "Frank's appetites also changed in that direction. He prefers the brains of his own kind, but since those are hard to come by, I substituted the brains of domesticated animals and he's been thriving on that."

Ariel runs her hand through her shampoo-commercial-perfect hair. "Monkey brains are eaten as a delicacy in some places. This isn't that different, I guess."

Yep. And that's the reason I only eat bananas when I'm on Earth.

Frank sticks his head out of the sack, the curious expression on his furry face seeming to say, "Did someone say yummy brains?"

"I can see why your people don't like to call them zombies." Itzel nods toward Rowan's helpers. "They want to save that term for where it's more applicable." She looks pointedly at Dylan.

With a growl, Fabian rushes over to where his clothes are, puts them on, and sprints over to Dylan.

Gently, he puts a hand on her shoulder.

Did Dylan just growl at him?

Nah. Must be my imagination.

"We did this to her," I whisper, looking up at Valerian.

His chiseled jaw tightens. "Don't beat yourself up. I was the one who pushed Rowan, and I'd do it again if I had to. So Dylan has an eccentric diet now. Still better than being dead."

The slurping noises stop, and Dylan stands up.

Fabian rips a chunk of cloth from the dead woman's nightgown and wipes the remnants of brain matter from Dylan's face.

"Thank you," Dylan says haltingly.

"Are you okay?" Ariel asks her, looking remarkably ungrossed out.

"I feel very strange." Dylan's tone is robotic, though a hint of her former intelligence glimmers in the empty pools of her eyes. "I see a lot of potential for research in this area, and that pleases me."

Uh-huh. Is she talking culinary research?

"We're going to get you a top-of-the-line laboratory," Valerian tells her. "Whatever you need. You'll be taken care of, I swear it."

Despite his earlier words, he must also feel guilty about his role in Dylan's fate.

Felix clears his throat. "If something happens to me, I want to go on record saying that I do *not* wish to be brought back like this. Maybe as a helper, if you really need one."

"Why would we need such a puny one?" Ariel retorts, and he sticks his tongue out at her.

Rowan glares at Valerian. "I'm not doing that again anyway. Not even with a gun to my head."

"Doing what?" Dylan asks.

No one replies, and Rowan sullenly collects her zombies.

"We'd better go," Valerian says and strides toward the next gate.

No one speaks, and nothing attacks us for the next two worlds.

When we get to the third hub, all seems quiet there as well. However, when we're halfway to the gate we need, the Overtaken leap out of the surrounding gates.

Puck.

Here we go again.

A cleaver flies at my shoulder.

I sidestep it and shoot the Overtaken responsible.

A wok careens at Valerian.

Double puck.

Valerian isn't dodging, nor am I going to be able to push him aside in time.

Smack. The wok hits one of Rowan's helpers in the head.

Whew. She must've made it jump in front of Valerian.

An Overtaken leaps at Fabian, an ax in his hands. Fabian dodges the weapon, then knocks his attacker out without bothering to shift into wolf form.

Ariel is attacked next. A blur of movement later, she has her opponent in a chokehold.

"Why don't I tell you about an interesting nightmare," says one of the Overtaken. "It all started—"

I shoot the speaker. "Don't listen to that," I tell the others urgently. "He's trying to plant the Overtaken nightmare into your subconscious."

"Bailey's right." Valerian's voice booms in my ears as though it's coming from the center of the universe. "I'll use my powers to block his future attempts, but if I forget or get knocked out, sing loudly or shove something into your ears."

"We can just shout *hoorah*," Ariel says, and does so as

she leaps at an Overtaken, knocking him out with a blow to the head.

"My turn," Rowan says and sics her entire undead army on our attackers.

I dodge a few more hits, but before long, our zombies triumph over the Overtaken, and we stun them again with our Gomorran guns.

Felix looks over the battlefield, then glances at the gates the Overtaken came from. "Did Phobetor take them over in each of those worlds?"

"Doubt it," Ariel says. "I bet they're local, and he had them exit through those gates to create an ambush. That's what I would've done."

"Right," Itzel mutters. "Let's hope he never overtakes you."

Amen to that.

Valerian's jaw tenses. "Either way you look at it, Collywobbles's vile influence is spreading."

I reach over and squeeze his forearm gently.

The tension drains out of his body as he looks at me, a now-familiar heat kindling in his gaze.

My breathing speeds up. This is so not the time for this.

As if to emphasize that, Dylan asks tonelessly, "Was it a dream, or did I eat a brain on the other world?"

Yep, that's a definite mood killer.

"You did," Fabian tells her softly. "But that's okay. In wolf form, I eat all the organs."

Dylan stares at him uncomprehendingly.

"You know what happened to you, right?" Fabian asks. "You know that Rowan—"

"I was dead, and now I'm not," Dylan says, sounding less robotic. "I think it's starting to sink in."

Valerian and I exchange a meaningful glance.

"The more you become your old self, the better," I say. Hopefully that also leads to fewer eaten brains, but I keep that to myself.

"Right," Dylan says distantly. "But who or what was my old self?"

Shooting Rowan a death glare, Fabian grabs Dylan's hand and drags her toward the next gate.

"Hold up," I say before they cross over. "The next world is the one where the Overtaken giants attacked us. Can we handle it if they do it again?"

They stop as Rowan scratches the jet-black side of her hairdo. "You killed them the last time, right?" she asks.

"We had no choice." Ariel glances at our current batch of unconscious attackers. "The guns don't stun giants."

"Not judging. In some situations, you don't have a choice." Rowan darts Fabian a dirty look. "I was just thinking that I might be able to recruit the bodies of your kills."

"They were mostly in pieces," Valerian says. "Besides, I'm sure their friends and family have buried their remains by now—and probably not by the gate."

Rowan takes out Frank and strokes his matted fur. "That's not good. Giants are powerful."

Valerian examines the knocked-out Overtaken in front of us. "We *could* make some more zombies for you."

"Dude," Felix says. "That's cold."

Ariel activates her gate sword. "I can take on a giant."

"Me too," Fabian growls.

"I have a better idea," I say and tell them what it is.

"It could work," Rowan says. "I can't help but notice that I'll be assuming all the risk, though."

Fabian crosses his arms over his chest. "Do you have a better plan? Maybe there's someone else's life you'd like to ruin?"

Rowan heaves a sigh and has the zombies gather in one group near our destination gate. Then she makes some of the smaller ones climb onto the shoulders of the bigger ones, thus forming zombie pyramids.

She then clasps the hands of the bottom zombies of two of the pyramids and leads them to the gate. When she gets there, she sticks her head and arms inside, which lets the zombies clear the gate completely.

Rowan herself stays without crossing, with only half her body in the world of the giants.

My hope is that she'll make a much smaller target for any attackers this way.

"Dude." Ariel tugs on the back of Felix's shirt. "Are you checking out Rowan's butt?"

Reddening, Felix shifts his gaze from Rowan's leather-clad posterior to his shoes. "It's not what you think. I was just—"

"Don't." Ariel grins. "I'm just looking out for you. You know how jealous Maya gets. You're so close to finally losing your virginity, I'd hate for you to blow it now."

Impossibly, Felix reddens more.

I suppress a grin. Maya is his young girlfriend, and I'm not sure it would be Earth legal for them to do what Ariel suggests. I also make a mental note to keep my lack of real-world sex experience to myself—I don't need Ariel to label me a virgin.

Especially since I probably won't stay one for long with Valerian around.

Suddenly, Rowan's body tenses.

I hurry toward her. "Rowan? Are you hurt?"

Valerian catches up to me. "I think she's fine."

Sure enough, Rowan pulls her arms out of the gate, grabs another set of zombie hands, and shepherds through yet another pyramid—all the while keeping her head in the giants' world.

Through all this, Felix keeps his gaze anywhere but on Rowan's tush.

When all the zombies have crossed over, I expect Rowan to return to us, but she maintains her stance, her muscles coiled tight, as if for battle.

Finally, she steps fully into the gate, which is our cue to follow.

When we come out on the other side, it's to a scene of a massacre.

Ninety percent of Rowan's zombies are in pieces on the ground. However, a dozen or so giants are unconscious too, and three appear to have been killed, because they're now zombies at Rowan's command.

"Once my helpers had smothered that one, I took him over as you suggested." Rowan gestures at the largest zombie giant. "Then I had him knock out his brethren, and when a few punches proved fatal by accident, I didn't let the bodies go to waste."

I dart a worried glance at Dylan.

There's a lot of brain matter scattered about.

To my relief, she's just looking around blankly. If she's got any cravings, she's not giving into them—a good sign.

Fabian sniffs the air and grabs Dylan in a fireman's carry. "We'd better leave before more giants arrive."

Sure enough, in the distance, near huts the size of four-story buildings, are new figures—and they're headed our way.

Without further delay, we sprint for our destination gate.

With a roar, the giants launch into a sprint as well, gaining on us quickly.

Ariel and Fabian, with Dylan draped over his shoulder, dive into the gate first, followed by Rowan and her remaining zombies.

"Hurry!" Valerian yells and all but throws me into the gate as the giants' pounding footsteps shake the ground around us.

Flying out the other side, I stumble, nearly faceplanting, but before I can panic about Valerian's fate, I feel his hands on my waist, steadying me.

"Everyone good?" Ariel asks, panting as we run for the next gate, and we all reply in the affirmative, not daring to slow down in case the giants have followed us in.

Around us is a green savannah with waist-high grass—not super conducive to a run, but we do our best. And it's a good thing, because thunderous sounds reach our ears and the grass around us vibrates as the ground shakes.

Did the giants follow us?

How many are there?

"Crap," Felix breathes. "It's those mammoths again."

Oh, right. On the way to Necronia, we nearly got trampled here.

"There!" Fabian points to our left.

Puck. The fierce mega creatures are stampeding our way once again.

Can Phobetor take over animals, or is this bad luck? Or did he Overtake a person who's scared these animals into running toward us?

No time to stick around and find out.

We further pick up our pace, but our target gate is too far.

"Rowan," I shout. "Slow them down!"

The necromancer is already on it. The biggest zombie giant lumbers forward and firmly plants his feet between us and the mammoths.

The herd smashes into him, sending him flying—but moments are all we need to leap into our destination gate.

———

THE NEXT WORLD LOOKS SAFE, but we rush through it anyway, in case the Overtaken jump out of the gates. Nothing attacks us, though. We clear the world after that without incident also, and same goes for the one with a toxic-looking green sky.

"No wonder Nostradamus got involved," Ariel says as we get to the following gate. "Phobetor—I mean, Collywobbles—seems to be a threat to everyone everywhere."

Itzel adjusts her gnome mask. "I wonder what his end goal is?"

"To kill me, that's for sure," I say. Then, realizing I never told them about the things Valerian and I discovered in his black windows, I do so, just glossing over the Soma bits since everything to do with that place is so hush-hush.

"So Nostradamus has shown up twice in your life," Ariel says, frowning. "That can't be good."

Felix's unibrow dances on his forehead. "I agree. What I don't understand is Collywobbles's actions. Even if killing you is one of his goals, there has to be more. Otherwise, why Overtake so many? Why start Icelus groups?"

Valerian squeezes my shoulder. "According to the lore of our people, his end goal is for every sentient being to end up in a state of perpetual nightmares. Thanks to Icelus activity, he's stronger than ever, and closer to realizing that objective."

We all mull this over until we get to a blue gate. It leads us to a never-ending desert with a strangely starless night sky and no Overtaken. The one after that is a gray tundra—again blissfully empty.

The next world is hotter than a bathhouse, with pterodactyl-like birds circling above us like vultures over a roadkill. When one dares to dive down, Rowan makes one of the giant zombies swat it away like a fly. After that, the rest of the birds decide to wait for easier prey.

"After the next world, we'll be on Gomorrah," I tell Rowan. "Earth is just a gate away from there."

The necromancer perks up, then gives Valerian a worried glance. No doubt she's wondering if he'll keep his promise to get her citizenship on Earth—especially in light of Dylan's new situation.

I'm pretty sure he will, but if he doesn't, I'll speak up on Rowan's behalf.

The pre-Gomorrah world has a fluorescent purple sky with pink cotton-candy clouds, a Saturn-like ring, and two moons.

Forgetting her worries, Rowan cranes her neck to stare at the heavens in openmouthed fascination.

We speed up, our steps lighter thanks to a difference in gravity.

"I don't think we should bring the zombies to Gomorrah," Valerian says, turning to Rowan. "In general, we can't have you stay there long—and what little time you spend there, you must keep your nature hidden. Vampires have a lot more pull on Gomorrah compared to Earth. They might well kill you first, then apologize after."

Rowan audibly swallows, and her zombies fall lifelessly to the ground.

I hadn't realized vampires had that much influence on Gomorrah, but Valerian is probably right. They're our police force and the army rolled into one.

Rowan definitely made the right choice with Earth.

We go through the gate.

At the sight of the Gomorrah skyline, Rowan's eyes widen to comical levels.

I can't blame her. It's cooler than all the Earth cities combined, and certainly bigger than anything I've seen on Necronia.

Valerian leads us away from the gates, then stops in the center of the skyscraper roof hub and begins making VR gestures in the air—probably checking on Senate business and summoning us a ride.

There aren't many people around, but something catches my attention in the periphery.

Heartbeat picking up, I spin around.

Five people step out of the gates nearest us.

Familiar people.

Four of them are former members of our Necronia delegation, and all five are on the New York Council.

There's Nina, a black-haired telekinetic with facial piercings; Kit, a shapeshifter who currently looks like her anime-character self; Chester, a probability manipulator with a satyr-like face; Colton, a rather tiny giant; and last and my least favorite, Gertrude, a gangrene giver who hates my guts for no good reason.

Felix and the others spot them too, and at first, they smile.

The smiles quickly turn into furrowed brows when they get a closer look.

Everyone but Gertrude sports the fiery eyes of the Overtaken.

CHAPTER FOUR

"HELLO AGAIN," Phobetor booms through Colton's giant throat. "Gertrude and I made a deal. I rid her of her sleep problems, and in exchange, she unlocked the bedrooms of your friends." Colton's mouth curves in a macabre grin. "How about you and I make a deal also? Hand over the dreamwalker, and I let you go."

Valerian responds with a rude gesture—hopefully speaking for everyone—and I narrow my eyes at Gertrude. The woman once came to me to solve her sleeping problem, and I couldn't. She sometimes kills people with her power when she sleepwalks, but still, working with Phobetor isn't a good solution.

It's a stupid one, in fact.

Valerian's thoughts must flow along the same lines. "Traitor," he mutters, glaring at her. "You'll lose your Council seat over this."

Gertrude smirks. "Who's going to tell them once you're dead?"

Eyes narrowing, Valerian shoots an arc of pulsing red energy into Gertrude's head.

The gangrene giver's pupils dilate, and her head swivels from side to side, her face a mask of horror. Whatever experience Valerian has just created for her must be bad, because she screams, as if in pain.

Is it wrong that I feel just a touch of joy at Gertrude's misfortune—or schadenfreude, as Fabian would call it?

"I take it you know this motley crew?" Rowan asks, surveying our opponents.

"We do, and that's the problem." I take out my gun and verify that it's still on a nonlethal setting. "We don't want to harm them."

"I'll take on Colton," Fabian growls. "A giant can take a few punches." He morphs into his wolf form, his clothes ripping into confetti in the process. With a howl, he rushes at Colton.

"I'll help," Ariel says, leaping after Fabian.

Dylan doesn't say anything, just follows Ariel and Fabian with halting steps.

Everything happens almost at once.

Chester runs at Rowan, while Kit morphs into a cheetah and leaps in Felix's direction. Itzel shoots a ball of lighting at Chester but misses. I shoot him with my gun and miss as well. Itzel throws another ball of lighting. Still misses.

Puck.

Chester's luck powers must be in play.

Fine. Felix needs help too.

I shoot at Kit, but my feet lift off the ground and I miss her as well.

Puck. There can be only one reason why I'm flying outside the dream world.

Nina's telekinesis.

I can't believe this is happening to me again.

Within seconds, I'm hovering five feet off the ground. Fighting nausea, I twist in the air until I'm upside down—and see Cheetah Kit mid-leap at Felix's throat.

Without aiming, I shoot twice.

Oops. Both Felix and Kit fall—but at least she never made it to his throat.

Nina lifts me another foot, and I flail desperately but without much to show for it. My breaths speed up. I think a part of me hopes I'll magically turn into a helium balloon that will stay up when Nina inevitably drops me.

Below me, Ariel grips Colton's right leg, and Dylan does the same to his left.

With another howl, Fabian smashes a paw into the giant's solar plexus.

Colton falls with a loud boom.

My relief mixes with concern. I hope Fabian was right, and Colton can handle this abuse.

My worry deepens when Chester reaches Rowan and knocks her out with a backhanded slap.

Nina lifts me another few feet. As I fly, I try flexing my core and twisting.

Score.

I'm facing the direction I want.

I aim my gun at Nina and do my best not to dwell on the fact that once I press the trigger, I'm going to plummet.

The hesitation costs me. The gun is wrenched out of my hand by a telekinetic pull, and a moment later, Nina's aiming it at me.

Gertrude's screams cease, and I see Valerian aiming his gun at Nina's head.

Nina collapses.

Valerian blurs into motion.

I drop like a granite statue of an obese elephant.

CHAPTER FIVE

I SQUEEZE my eyes shut so I don't see the ground rush toward me. If I were a cat, I'd twist in the air so I can land on my feet. Then again, wouldn't that break my feet? My heart tries to evacuate my body through my throat, and I can't exactly blame it.

I land on something hard, but in a strange way, with my butt sinking deeper.

I open my eyes.

Valerian's face is above me. He's caught me in his outstretched arms.

He's saying something soothing, but the hammering pulse in my ears makes it hard to make out his words.

Gently, he sets me on my feet. I grip his biceps as I catch my breath and scan the battle scene.

Colton is unconscious or worse, and Chester must've knocked out Itzel after he was done with Rowan because the gnome is lying there, unmoving.

Gertrude is on the floor, whimpering, and Chester is near her, fighting the trio of Ariel, Dylan, and Fabian.

To my utter astonishment, Chester is holding his own. Without super strength or speed, he's able to dodge Fabian's wolfu moves, as well as Ariel's lightning-fast kicks and punches. When Dylan occasionally tries to grab Chester, she doesn't succeed either.

Valerian aims his gun at Chester. Nothing happens. Valerian curses. There's an error code on the gun's screen, something about it needing a battery recharge.

Probability manipulation is a useful power.

"Can't you use an illusion on him?" I ask urgently when Chester dodges yet another round of attacks. "You can handle a single Overtaken, can't you? Without his other minions, Phobetor won't know what the true reality is."

"Let me try." Valerian points his hand at Chester.

"Wait. You need to show him something pleasant and fun. Something his powers will welcome."

Nodding, Valerian shoots his energy at Chester's head.

At first, Phobetor screams obscenities through Chester's lips. Then the fire disappears from Chester's eyes, and a dopey grin contorts his face, making him look even more like a puck or a satyr.

The crazy thing is that Ariel still misses when she tries to punch him in the face. Same goes for Dylan and Fabian.

"I got him," Valerian yells to them. "He won't fight back."

He's right. When Ariel and Fabian stop, Chester keeps standing there, absorbed in whatever pleasant vision Valerian has put him in.

Suddenly, there's a blur of movement at Fabian's feet—and blood ices over in my veins as I realize what it is.

CHAPTER SIX

GERTRUDE GRABS FABIAN'S hind paw.

Puck. How did we forget about her?

The rot is instant. Within an eyeblink, Fabian's leg looks as if it's been infected for weeks.

He licks the poor leg, then begins to howl. The gangrene spreads and spreads, until his howling turns to whimpers... and ceases.

No. Can't be. Please—

Fabian collapses in a rotten heap.

Dylan stares at Gertrude's hand, then glares unblinkingly at what's left of Fabian. Finally, her eyes narrow on Gertrude's throat, and a terrifying expression appears on her previously blank face.

"You want to be next?" Gertrude asks hoarsely.

Dylan lunges.

Ariel tries to catch her, but it's too late.

Dylan's hands are already squeezing Gertrude's throat.

In a moment, she'll be a rotting pile, like Fabian.

CHAPTER SEVEN

EXCEPT DYLAN'S hands don't rot. Her knuckles whiten as she squeezes Gertrude's throat, and that's it.

"Must be a side effect of her resurrected state," Ariel mutters in awe.

That makes some macabre sense. Gangrene happens when tissues die, but Dylan's tissues have been there, done that.

Realizing that her powers are useless, Gertrude flails. Dylan gives her a vicious jerk, smashing the back of her head into the roof. Gertrude's body goes limp. Dylan bashes her head into the roof again and again. Eventually, the gangrene giver's skull breaks.

I look away as slurping sounds begin.

Catching Valerian's gaze, I debate if I want him to blot out my senses.

"Serves Gertrude right," he says coldly. "Don't feel bad for her."

Seeing my miserable expression, he envelops me in

a tight hug, and we stand like that while a montage of my interactions with Fabian plays in my mind. I haven't known the werewolf for long, but we've been through so much together that I've grown to think of him as a friend.

If not for his selfless bravery, I might not be alive today.

"Did he have any family?" I whisper, my voice catching as I lean deeper into the hug.

Valerian's lips brush my ear. "Don't worry about them. The Councils will take care of everything."

Swallowing the lump in my throat, I pull away.

I have to check on my friends.

Ariel must be on the same wavelength. She's already kneeling next to Itzel. Seeing my concerned expression, she gives me a thumbs up. "Felix is just out as well," she says. "And Rowan will live. Same goes for the giant."

A Colton-sized weight lifts off my shoulders, even as my gaze finds the pile that was Fabian, and dark anger surges through me.

I thought I hated Phobetor before, but I didn't understand the subtleties of hate until now. It's heart-wrenching to see Dylan standing over Fabian's remains, looking completely lost. She must've felt something for him, something that transcended her resurrection. And now she's lost him.

I look at Valerian, and my heart squeezes painfully in my chest.

I could've lost him too.

I still might.

"I'll take Dylan to Earth and get her settled," Valerian says. "You focus on your mother."

My mom. Of course. I almost—

A flying car lands on the roof.

"If that's more Overtaken, I give up," I mutter.

Fortunately, it's not.

Virgil, a vampire I've met before, comes out of the car, along with a score of other Enforcers.

Vampires don't need to sleep, so I doubt they make good targets for Phobetor.

"These Overtaken need to be taken back to the New York Council," Valerian tells Virgil.

"And Felix needs medical care," I say.

Valerian nods. "I'll take them all to Earth."

"What about him?" Virgil looks questioningly at Chester, who's still standing there, staring at some alternate reality brought about by Valerian's powers.

"That's one of the reasons I'm coming with you," Valerian says.

I bite my lip, staring at him. "I want to be with you." It's illogical, irrational, but I can't help the feeling that if he leaves, I might never see him again.

"What about your mom?" he asks. "Besides, I just got a message. There's a pandemic on Earth. A virus. And though it's not as deadly as the one we've just been cured from, I know how you feel about germs, and there isn't a treatment so far, so…"

I stare at him in horror. "Did Icelus cause this pandemic too?"

"No evidence of that," he says. "Might just be a coincidence—but it benefits Collywobbles nevertheless. With no treatment in sight and billions of lives at risk, there'll be plenty of nightmares for him to feast on."

Dylan looks up from her grisly meal. Her eyes are glimmering with pain and a fraction of her old intelligence. "A virus?"

Valerian tilts his head. "If you're interested, I'll make sure you have whatever you need to develop a treatment or a vaccine."

Dylan wipes what must be bits of Gertrude's brain from her mouth with a sleeve. "I think I'd better focus on my impulse control and dietary requirements first and foremost."

Smart. It wouldn't help anyone if she accidentally ate the brain of a colleague.

Valerian locks eyes with me. "I'll come back as soon as I can."

I almost ask him to take me with him, virus be damned.

But no. I can't delay visiting Mom's dreams any longer.

"Be careful," I tell him, and he smiles.

"We have hazmat suits waiting, don't worry."

"Fine. I give you two hours," I say gruffly. "Three at the most."

"Your wish is my command," he says, and stepping up to me, he slants his mouth over mine.

My body instantly ignites. Mighty hormones, what

is he doing to me? The world around us disappears as fireworks explode in my belly—and maybe in the sky.

"There's no time for that," Dylan's voice says from somewhere.

Ugh. Can't she just go and eat another brain so we can have a moment?

To my immense disappointment, Valerian pulls away.

"To be continued," he says with a cocky smirk.

Virgil strides over, Itzel in bridal carry in his arms.

All amusement vanishes from Valerian's face, and he narrows his eyes at the vampire. "If something happens to Bailey, I will hold you personally responsible. Understand?"

"We've taken all the precautions," Virgil says. "Everyone around her with the exception of the gnome doctor will be a vampire. Even though we don't need to sleep, some of us choose to do so on occasion, but I've forbidden everyone from dreaming until this whole mess is resolved. The new safe house is a veritable bunker that no—"

"Just know that your existences are intertwined," Valerian says grimly. "This isn't just me speaking. She's the highest priority for the Senate."

I am?

Virgil nods. "Let's go."

I don't move. I guess I still haven't fully recovered my wits.

Valerian grabs my hand and shepherds me to the flying car.

Virgil slides Itzel onto the seat next to me, while Valerian kisses me once more, then closes the door before I can clutch his shirt and refuse to let go.

As the car ascends, I spot Felix sitting up.

He's definitely okay.

We torpedo forward, accompanied by a squadron of flying cars.

"My team," Virgil explains when he sees my concerned glance at the other vehicles.

After we traverse a couple of city blocks, Itzel comes to her senses and peppers me with questions about what happened after she passed out. As I explain, Virgil listens on, but keeps his expression blank. My voice cracks as I tell Itzel about Fabian's demise, and we fly the rest of the way in a mournful silence.

When we reach the southernmost district of Gomorrah City, we land on a roof of a mega skyscraper I've never visited before. Virgil leads us to an elevator, where he swipes his comms over a special reader, and we begin to descend. And keep descending for an obscenely long time.

If we step out into the iron core of the planet, I won't be surprised.

I turn to Virgil. "When you mentioned a bunker, you meant it literally, didn't you?"

He nods. "The Senate built it a while back for themselves. Valerian convinced them to let us use it for a while."

The elevator finally stops, and when the doors

open, it's to a room filled to the brim with vampires, all dressed in riot gear and armed to the teeth.

One of them hands Itzel some strange headgear contraption and steps back, aiming a gun at the poor gnome. "Put it on."

"What is that?" I ask.

The vampire who provided the contraption looks at Virgil.

"That's a security measure," Virgil says patiently. "Though we haven't seen a single Overtaken gnome, it doesn't hurt to be careful. This device will detect it if you fall sleep—and it'll alert the team."

Itzel takes the gizmo, examines it approvingly, and puts it on her head like a crown. "It's gnome designed, isn't it?"

"Indeed," says a familiar voice from behind a wall of vampires. "I made it."

The vampires let the gnome through.

He's wearing the same headgear as Itzel, and I recognize him instantly.

It's Mom's doctor.

"Hi, Dr. Xipil," I say. "Let me introduce you to Itzel."

Itzel extends her small hand in an almost coquettish manner. "A pleasure."

A smile touches the corners of Dr. Xipil's eyes as he shakes the proffered hand. "The pleasure is all mine. I've done much in the past few weeks that I wanted a fellow gnome to appreciate."

Itzel points at her head. "That's some interesting

work. And I've never met a gnome doctor before. What made—"

"How about you flirt on the way?" Virgil says with an eye roll, then herds me and the chatty pair down a corridor. A labyrinthine walk later, we enter a large room where another strange contraption stands, with Mom inside it.

If Felix's old robot suit had a baby with a hospital bed, and if that baby mated with a tank, this is what the offspring would look like.

"That's my pride and joy," Dr. Xipil says. "Valerian wanted to make sure your mother is safe, and can be moved around freely. My design was inspired by—"

"Does it open?" I cut in, my eyes not leaving Mom's placid face behind the thick glass. "I need to touch her for what comes next."

Nodding, Dr. Xipil takes out a remote screen and hits a few icons on it.

The contraption rolls up to us, and the thick glass opens like a clam shell.

"Amazing work," Itzel says, but I'm no longer paying attention to her. Walking over to Mom, I place my fingers on her forehead. Two questions swirl through my mind as I prepare to use my powers.

Is it finally going to happen? Will I be able to bring her out of the coma?

CHAPTER EIGHT

EVEN WITHOUT DR. XIPIL'S equipment, my senses tell me Mom isn't in REM sleep. That means that if I were to simply jump into her dreams, I'd end up in a subdream and risk my sanity.

Why do that if I can put people into REM sleep with my powers?

I try that now, but it doesn't work.

Odd.

I attempt it again. Still nothing.

"Is she on any stimulants?" I ask Dr. Xipil, interrupting his bragging.

"No. Why?"

"I can now put people into REM sleep, except it's not working on her."

"No stimulants," Dr. Xipil says. "Just fluids and nutrients."

Itzel's eyebrows furrow. "Could your powers be malfunctioning after all that stress?"

"Lie down on the floor," I tell her.

"What?" The gnome steps back, but Virgil is already in her way.

"I'm just going to test my powers on you," I say. "Please."

Reluctantly, Itzel lies on the floor.

"Her hat is about to tell you she's asleep," I tell Virgil. "Make sure your people don't panic."

With a loud sigh, Virgil makes a few gestures in his VR.

"Don't fight it. I need your consent," I tell Itzel, and she sighs before nodding in agreement.

I bend down, touch her forehead, and do the exact same push as a second ago.

Itzel is in REM sleep instantly, and her headgear begins to buzz and flash with lights, waking her up.

I wince, rubbing my ears. "Seems like this hat is an alarm in more ways than one."

Virgil shrugs. "Waking up is preferable to what my team and I might do to a suspected Overtaken."

Itzel sits up. "I started to have a very nice dream," she says groggily, then looks up at Dr. Xipil. "You were there."

"Were you playing doctor?" Virgil asks.

Itzel gets up, her ears reddening.

Having made sure my powers are in good working order, I try to push Mom into REM sleep once again.

It still doesn't work.

I turn to Dr. Xipil. "Do you have something that can put her into REM sleep?"

He shakes his head.

I face Virgil. "Do we have any of that Koshmar drug the Icelus use?"

"I wouldn't recommend giving that to Lidia," Dr. Xipil says sternly.

"We don't have it anyway," Virgil says.

I scratch my chin. "What about Maxwell?"

"Who?" Dr. Xipil asks.

"Another dreamwalker," Virgil says. "What about him?"

"Can you bring him over here?" I ask. "Maybe he can do this?"

Virgil makes VR gestures again. "My people are on it."

Belatedly, I recall my suspicion that there was more to Maxwell than met the eye. At the time, I thought he was the Nutcracker, but that turned out to be Rattie.

Still, is it safe to have him so close to me and Mom?

"Keep an eye on him when he comes," I tell Virgil. "Give him one of those hats too."

Virgil flashes his fangs. "You don't need to tell me how to do my job."

Just my luck. I'm stuck in the middle of the planet's core with a thin-skinned vampire.

"Is there a place I can sit as I wait?" I ask.

Virgil leads me into something like a waiting room, while Itzel and Dr. Xipil remain behind, chatting about their designs.

Getting comfortable in a chair, I touch's Pom's fur

and, with the familiar falling sensation and a whiff of ozone, enter the dream world.

———

WHEN I SHOW up in my impossibly colored, manna-scented palace lobby, Pom is standing in front of a pyre of wooden logs, holding a lit match.

"Playing with fire?" I ask.

The pyre and the matches disappear, and Pom's fur turns a deep purple. "You're here! I've missed you. What's new?"

He seems so happy that I'm loath to tell him about the recent events. But he insists, so I recount everything.

By the time I'm done, Pom's fur is a washed-out gray. "I don't like Phobetor. He's a major meanie."

"I'd use much stronger language, but I agree with the sentiment." I stroke his head until his triangular ears regain a hint of purple.

"Can we play again?" he asks, blinking his huge lavender eyes at me.

"Does practice count as play?"

He turns a golden hue. "I think it does. Depends on what we're practicing."

I change our surroundings to a recreation of the environment where subdream battles occur.

An ocean of black water is now under our feet, and a magma sky is above. Not for the first time I notice that the sky is a lot like the eyes of the Overtaken—and the water is not that different from the kind inside the black windows, except I have no problem standing on subdream water.

Pom warily examines the new environment. "What kind of practice did you have in mind?"

"If Maxwell doesn't know how to put Mom into REM sleep, I'll have to get to her via the subdream again. It occurred to me that we can practice some skills that might help us survive in that scenario."

Pom's ears wiggle slightly. "How would that work?"

"I'm making this up as we go. For starters, do you think you could somehow realize a subdream is a subdream and tell me?"

His ears droop and take on a beet color. "Every subdream looks like this, yet I don't realize it. Too lost, like your clients before you tell them they're dreaming."

"The same happens to me. Maybe if we hang around here long enough and keep reiterating that this is where subdreams take place, something will stick?"

He perks up. "Maybe. Also, you're a more powerful dreamwalker now. Maybe that'll help you the next time."

I sigh. "I hope so."

"So we just run around here?" His ears take on a carrot hue. "That doesn't sound like fun."

"You know how you've been turning into weapons for me when subdreams happen?"

His fur turns brown, and he lifts his chin. "I do it instinctively. It's what saves our lives."

"Exactly. And you've been all kinds of different

weapons. But I think my preference would be a katana."

Pom leaps at my wrist and becomes a bracelet, as if this were the waking world. He then extends and turns into a furry blade.

I touch the edge of the Pom katana, and my finger starts bleeding. In this form, my symbiont is surprisingly sharp.

I slash the furry katana through the air a few times. "This is awesome. Let's practice you doing that. Hopefully you'll get so used to it you'll do the same in the subdream."

Pom separates from my wrist and expands until he becomes his cute self again. "To make it more fun, we need something for you to slay."

Genius.

I manifest a creature that attacked us in a subdream once. It looks like twenty ant mandibles grew to the size of a truck, then sprouted antennae and legs.

Pom shudders. "Creepy. Could probably also work as exposure therapy."

"Less talking and more turning into a katana, please."

With a grin, he leaps onto my wrist again, then extends and becomes the blade I favor.

I jump up and slice the mandible creature's head clean off. As it evaporates, I remind myself that monsters plus black ocean and fiery skies means a subdream. I want it to become a strong enough association that I might think of it when in a real subdream.

Pom transforms back into himself. "That was fun. Let's do it again."

This time, our opponent resembles a giant spiral worm—or syphilis bacteria, but with centipede-like legs ending in knife-sharp talons.

As soon as Pom becomes the katana, I behead the spiral worm with a flick of my wrist.

My looft is right. This is kind of fun.

Wait, almost forgot to remind myself that this is what a subdream looks like.

Before Pom can stop being a blade, I bring forth another monster from our subdream past—a ten-foot-tall monstrosity that reminds me of a tardigrade, a micro animal that lives in water, has no discernible eyes or nose, a hole for a mouth, and eight limbs that end in claws attached to a fat, sea-cow-like body.

Leaping off the water, I somersault in the air as I swing Pom.

Tardigrade's head separates from its body.

This is a subdream. The thought pops into my head almost on autopilot this time—a great sign.

As I'm landing, I create the next target: a hairless and earless humanoid figure with one huge mouth where the face should be. It's got a sword-like claw growing out of its right index finger, and I make it take a swing at me. I dodge the strike, then behead it like the others—while reminding myself of subdreams.

Now I'm really getting into the spirit of this exercise.

I recreate another monster I've met in subdreams, a pair in fact: a mount that looks like a warthog crossed with a spider and its rider, a giant naked mole rat with tentacles.

I leap off the water and swing my sword once, twice.

Both the warthog mount and the mole rat rider lose their heads at the same time.

"Subdream," I mutter.

Pom morphs into a talking version of himself. "These are so scary, yet I'm okay."

I grin at him. "The exercise is working. Now if only it were this easy in the real subdream."

Shrugging, Pom becomes a katana again.

I make our next opponent a turkey vulture, only skeletal and covered in pustules, with a featherless body and claws. Feeling bold, I let the monster fly at me while I wait in a samurai stance, with Pom above my head.

The vulture dives. As I wait, I think the magic word: *subdream*. Just as the vulture's claws are ready to rip into my flesh, I slice.

Score. Another successful beheading.

I create more creatures and practice beheading them, all the while repeating the phrase "this is a subdream" like a mantra.

For the next phase of the training, I animate the monsters and make them even more aggressive with their attacks. Next, I create them in groups—first pairing the tardigrade with the nail-sword thing, then the ant with the spiral worm, then the vulture with the warthog and its ugly rider. Finally, I throw them all into a fight and behead them until my Pom katana feels like a real extension of my hand.

The world around me vibrates.

Someone is trying to wake me from my trance in the real world.

"Pom, train without me for a bit," I say and jolt myself awake.

———

I WAKE to the sight of Virgil's pale face a foot away from mine.

"What?" The question come out sharper than is wise when dealing with a killing machine that is a vampire.

To my relief, he doesn't bat an eye at my rudeness. "Maxwell has arrived. Shall I take you to see him?"

I stand up, eager to see the other dreamwalker. "Let's go."

Virgil leads me down a corridor. Stopping next to a metal door, he unlocks it and ushers me in.

There's a man inside.

I stare at him.

Specifically, at his familiar features.

"Is this a... a joke?" I stammer.

Virgil frowns at me uncomprehendingly, and so does the man.

"Valerian?" I spin in a circle. "Is it you doing this?"

Virgil presses his finger to his temple and makes a circling motion.

The man is also looking at me like I've gone crazy. "I'm Maxwell," he says slowly.

His voice is also familiar, and not from when we met near Necronia. That time, it had been out of context and muffled by his mask, so nothing had clicked. That same mask had also concealed his features—just as my mask must've concealed mine, preventing him from recognizing me.

But now he *should* know who I am. Yet he's acting as if we're strangers.

"Don't you recognize me?" I ask breathlessly. "I'm Bailey."

"I figured." Maxwell stares at me with a deepening frown. "You do look vaguely familiar, though I've only seen you in a mask. In fact—" His face twists. "No, I can't place it, I'm sorry."

He can't, but I can.

Because I saw him recently without a mask, and more than once.

It was in Mom's black window memories, and Valerian's as well.

Maxwell isn't just a random dreamwalker.

He's my father.

CHAPTER NINE

I WANT to lunge forward and embrace him. I also want to lash out, yelling questions like "where the puck have you been all my life?" and "why don't you recognize your own daughter?"

But I don't say anything.

I can guess what happened. He's forgotten me, same as Mom has forgotten Asha, my twin, and for the same reason. Soma illusionists made him—and Phobetor, who took him over—think that he killed me.

Yet even if I'm right, it doesn't make this feel any better. His lack of recognition feels too much like rejection. Like I don't matter to him... which I guess I don't.

Maxwell nervously brushes the gray stubble on his chin. "Bailey, is everything okay? You look upset."

I pull myself together, ignoring the pitch-black Pom on my wrist. "There's a dreamwalking problem I need your help with," I say, my voice impressively even.

His amber eyes brighten. "What's the problem?"

"It's my mother. Her name is Lidia."

He shows almost no reaction to the name, except maybe a slight widening of his pupils.

Seems like he's forgotten more than just little old me.

Could he be missing all the memories related to Soma, like Valerian was? If so, he wouldn't even recognize Mom—assuming Soma is where they met.

"She's in a coma," I continue and explain the strange state Mom is stuck in and how I need to push her into REM sleep so I can jolt her awake from inside her dream world.

"Sure, I can try to put her into REM sleep." He rakes a hand through his salt-and-pepper hair. "Where is she?"

I glance at Virgil, who turns around and leads us down the corridor.

The two gnomes are still in Mom's room, still chatting after all this time. I ignore them, my attention on my father's face as he looks at Mom.

"Have you met her before?" I ask, gesturing at the rolling-bed contraption. "She's a dreamwalker like us."

Maxwell stares at her, his forehead creasing. "She does look familiar…" Stepping closer, he scans her face. "The two of you share some features."

So that's that. He's missing *a lot* of memories.

Knowing that I'm not the only one he's forgotten should make me feel better, but it doesn't. All I feel is sadness… and under it, my anger at Phobetor expands. He's pucked up the lives of everyone in my family.

He's torn us apart.

Reining in my emotions, I ask, "Do you need to touch her? I saw you do this from afar with Dylan…"

Maxwell keeps staring at Mom's face as if he's planning to carve a statue of her later. "Doing it with touch is the more conservative approach," he responds absentmindedly.

Dr. Xipil opens the clamshell again, and Maxwell hesitantly reaches out, placing his hand on Mom's wrist.

Closing his eyes, he stands there for a few seconds. Then he opens his eyes and gives me a regretful look. "I'm sorry. It didn't work for me either."

Puck. "Would it help if we did it together?"

He shrugs. "Doesn't hurt to try."

I walk over and touch Mom's other wrist.

This time, we both close our eyes and push.

Nope. Even with our joint effort, Mom doesn't go into REM sleep.

I open my eyes. "I guess I'm going in as is." Hopefully all that training with Pom will help.

Maxwell jerks his hand away, eyeing me like I've already been killed in the subdream and have gone homicidally crazy. "You can't."

I lift an eyebrow.

"It's extremely dangerous. If you get—"

"I've done it many times," I say curtly. "I know what to expect."

"But—"

"I appreciate your concern. How about you wait behind Virgil… just in case."

Taking it as his cue, Virgil strides over.

"If I try to kill you, you have my permission to restrain me," I tell him.

Virgil grimaces. "How about you wait until Valerian is back? If I do have to restrain you, you could get hurt. I don't want an awkward conversation with your lover."

I flush.

I wish Valerian were really that.

Maxwell looks even more worried now. "Don't do this, Bailey. Can't Lidia get to REM sleep on her own?"

Dr. Xipil clears his throat. "That never happens."

"I'm going in," I say firmly. "Don't distract me."

Before anyone can stop me, I grasp Mom's wrist and dive in.

CHAPTER TEN

SOMETHING IS VAGUELY familiar about the black water under my feet and the magma sky.

A gang of creatures is attacking. Their bodies are semi-humanoid, but their heads don't even try—with rows of shark teeth, small beady eyes, and a tentacle with a light on its tip, these heads look like they belong to anglerfish, or some other deep-water monstrosity.

Shouldn't these guys live under this ocean? No time to figure it out. One of the anglers is almost upon me.

A furry appendage snakes from my wrist and turns into a katana.

Something feels right about the whole situation. The katana feels natural, like a best friend.

The closest angler screeches in a voice as ugly as its face, "You're the one the master hates!"

I teach it the mistake of chatting during a battle. With a whirl of my katana, the fishy head is separated from the body.

"Your existence is a blight!" the next one screeches as it leaps at me.

Whoosh. Another head severed.

Without any further talking, the rest of them attack en masse. A claw scratches my cheek. I yelp in pain and behead the attacker almost on autopilot. Saber-like teeth tear into my left shoulder. Ignoring the pain, I swing my katana. The biter is no more.

The rest circle around me warily, no doubt biding time until I weaken from the blood loss, which sadly isn't going to take long.

Desperate, I go on the offensive. With a leap, I behead the largest surviving angler and, landing on the ocean water, take a samurai stance.

The rest of the anglers back away. When I rush at one, it retreats faster. I don't give it chase because I'm feeling more and more faint. My shoulder is bleeding too much. I have minutes, maybe seconds before I faint —which is when they'll pounce.

Puck. I'm screwed, and they know it.

There's got to be something I can do.

It's on the tip of my tongue—or mind. Something about this scenario. Something about this sword. Something I trained myself to remember.

Wait. I trained *with* someone.

My eyes drop to my furry katana, and it finally clicks.

That's Pom—and since he isn't a bracelet on my wrist, I must be dreaming.

That's it.

Not that this is a dream, exactly. It's a subdream, and for the first time in my life, I'm aware of the fact that I'm here.

Giddily, I test out my usual powers by leaving my body.

It works!

I effortlessly heal myself, then jump back in.

The beady eyes of the anglers widen, and their retreat speeds up.

"Pom," I say to the katana. "You know this is a dream, right?"

At first, nothing happens. Then the blade morphs into Pom's usual dream form. His fur is black and his eyes wild as he takes in the anglers before poofing out of existence.

I can't blame him. This is almost too scary for me.

Oh well. Now that I have my powers, I manifest another katana in my hands.

The anglers turn and flee.

Taking to the air, I torpedo at the nearest angler and turn it into mincemeat without breaking a sweat. Grinning, I point my hand at my next victim and simply wish him out of existence. Then I land and dispatch another one. And another.

Then something odd happens.

A presence slowly congeals out of nothingness to stand on the ocean in front of me.

It's the nightmarish being I've seen before.

Phobetor.

CHAPTER ELEVEN

BIGGER THAN THE TALLEST GIANT, he's the most frightening thing I've ever seen—even if it's hard to say why. There's something ineffably horrific about him. Something that I feel with my dreamwalker senses instead of my vision. His face is actually beautiful, if in a terrible, overwhelming way that doesn't seem to be meant for mortal sight. Maybe it's his eyes. They look like black holes that contain every nightmare anyone has ever had. Looking into them is like walking in a dark forest as a child. Like having germs multiply inside your body. Like—

"Kneel." Phobetor's melodious voice conjures my every fear. "Become my servant."

Every cell in my body demands that I give in. In his embrace, there will be peace. Mom and I will reunite. I'll no longer feel this overwhelming fear. I'll—

"Puck. You," I grit out as I use all my power to throw off whatever spell he's trying to cast on me.

The black holes that are his eyes widen before narrowing dangerously. "Those who don't join me willingly, I can claim by force."

He advances toward me, hand outstretched.

There's a fiery flash in the magma sky above me, spiraling down.

A deep intuition tells me that if that tendril were to reach my head, that would be it. I would be one of the Overtaken.

Backing away, I hurl my katana at his face.

The blade melts and evaporates before it gets halfway to its destination, but killing him wasn't my goal anyway. I just wanted to distract him long enough to jolt myself awake.

It's the biggest jolt I've ever created.

And, to my shock, it works.

———

OPENING MY EYES, I jerk my hand away from Mom's wrist.

I'm not ready to go back.

Maybe I'll never be.

"Do I need to restrain you?" Virgil asks. "Valerian is on his way here, so I'd rather not."

My frantic heartbeat eases. "He is?"

Virgil's smile shows off his fangs. "He's just arrived at the hub. My people are picking him up."

I wipe the sweat from my forehead. "I guess I won't go on a killing spree then. As tempting as it is."

"That was reckless," Maxwell says sternly. "You could've—"

"There's something you need to know," I blurt.

He frowns in a way I've sometimes seen in the mirror.

"It's private," I say. "We should talk in the dream world." I cast an apologetic look at Dr. Xipil and Itzel, but don't bother with Virgil.

Maxwell's frown deepens. "Your dream world or mine?"

"How about yours," I say, feigning a casual attitude.

In fact, it must be his. My aim is to check his dreams for the presence of black windows—but I don't tell him this in case he's touchy about this topic, like Mom was.

Maxwell surveys the room. "Is there a bed around here?"

"This way." Virgil leads us into a room with a gurney and a wheelchair next to it.

What is this, a horror movie set?

Getting on the gurney, Maxwell extends his hand.

I take a seat in the wheelchair, clasp his fingers, and try to push him into REM sleep without further ado.

For a second, I worry that it might not work, like it didn't with Mom. But it does. His eyes start moving under his eyelids, and I can feel him in REM sleep with my special sense.

"This will be safer, so no need for subduing," I tell Virgil.

The vampire cocks his head. "So if you attack me, I should just let you?"

"Anything to avoid that awkward conversation with Valerian," I say and jump in.

I APPEAR in my dream palace in front of Pom.

My loolt's ears are beet-colored while the rest of him is gray. "I'm sorry I left during the subdream. I got too scared."

I pet the fur on the top of his head. "I also bailed—and for pretty much the same reason."

He gives me a quizzical look, and I tell him what happened as I make my way to the tower of sleepers.

When I locate my father, I tell Pom, "You can join this, but please stay incognito. Explaining you isn't on the agenda."

He leaps onto my shoulder and becomes invisible. *If we need to talk, let's do it mentally.*

Making myself invisible as well, I reach out and grab my father's wrist.

RIGHT AWAY, my senses inform me that this dream is a memory.

I let it play out, curious about my father's life.

He's sitting on the floor next to a coffee table in the middle of a sea of empty food containers, beer bottles, and piles of newspapers that span many years. The rest of the living room reminds me of Earth shows set in the fifties—with a tiny TV that looks like an astronaut's helmet, a phone with a cord attaching it to the wall, and uncomfortable furniture that was brightly colored once but is washed out now.

Maxwell is either playing solitaire or randomly moving playing cards around the table. His movements are sluggish, his expression that of bored despair.

Is he suffering despite having blocked out the painful memories? Pom mentally asks. *I think that's what happened to Lidia.*

This is just one dream, I reply. *Besides, this could just be the way life was before internet was invented.*

Despite my words, I suspect that Pom is right. This Maxwell seems like a broken man—and it's not unreasonable to think that his past is the cause.

Remembering my original goal, I look at the dusty shades blocking the two windows.

Hard to say if the glass behind the shades is black.

Moving softly to avoid detection, I walk over to one of the shades and lift it up. The city outside is dirty and dark, the building across covered in worn-out graffiti and rust streaks.

I walk over to the second window.

Not surprisingly, underneath this shade is black glass.

Suddenly, I become visible, and a voice booms through the room as though from a giant speaker. "Just what do you think you're doing?"

Okay. It's official. He's as touchy about this as Mom.

I feel myself jerked away from the black window and dragged five feet in my father's direction.

Pom's feet dig into my shoulder. He might be about to bolt.

"Maxwell, this is Bailey," I say soothingly. "We decided to have a talk in the dream world. Remember?"

He thrusts his hand at the black window, and metal blinds with spikes appear there, hiding it from view. "I don't remember giving you permission to sneak around."

I gesture at the metal blinds, and they melt into a puddle on the floor. "That black window is what I came to talk to you about."

"No!" He makes a sweeping gesture, and all the objects in the room fly at me.

Pom's feet are no longer on my shoulder.

As I suspected, he's found this too scary.

I try not to tense up as I increase the gravity in the room, causing all the projectiles to drop before reaching me.

Immediately, they rise up off the floor. I put them down again and round on Maxwell. "Stop fighting me! It's time for you to remember what you forgot."

His nostrils flare as he gestures at me, and I feel myself getting wrenched from the dream world.

Though I've never countered such an attack, I *have* forced myself to stay in the dream world through sheer willpower, and I do so now.

With a growl, he tries to jolt himself awake. I can feel him doing it.

Puck.

Remembering that the Nutcracker—Rattie—was able to prevent me from jolting, I do my best to guess how he did it. Maxwell's breathing grows louder, and he begins to sweat as I strain my powers, keeping him in the dream world with everything I've got.

Panting, he loosens his collar. "I don't want to harm you."

I grit my teeth. "More like you can't. Let's just go into that window. You'll see that I—"

He flexes and unflexes his fingers, and I get drenched with something like liquid nitrogen. The frostbite that covers my body feels like a burn—though that could in part be because I'm sizzling with anger.

Maxwell looms over me. "The only way I'm going into that window is if—"

I exit my body, but instead of healing, I create two duplicates of myself right behind Maxwell and jump into their bodies.

By the time his eyes widen, we already have him in our grasp.

He tries jolting awake again, but it's too late.

We all smash into the black glass.

CHAPTER TWELVE

AS USUAL, I plunge into icy black water.

There's only one of me here; the other remains in the room we were just in. Since I don't need to be in that room, I dispel that me and focus on my surroundings. Just like when I did this with Valerian, there's a rope attaching me to a rickety boat.

Inside is Maxwell.

If I make it to the shore, he's going to recall whatever this black window is blocking.

With no shore in sight, I swim.

After what feels like two days, my every muscle screams in pain, and the irritation from the rope burns is about to drive me mad.

Ignoring it all, I keep swimming. I remind myself this isn't real. This is just a trial of my strength, a way to make sure only the worthy can give my father his memory back.

Well, I'm worthy. If I was able to give back the

memories of Soma to Valerian, I should be able to do this too.

Soon, swimming becomes a type of water-based yoga, my breath and movements synchronized perfectly and my mind purely in present moment.

This helps for a few hours, but then thoughts of quitting return. To battle them, I glance back at Maxwell's face and fantasize about how it'll look when he learns the truth.

This keeps me going for what feels like another day.

At some point, the exhaustion and pain grow completely unbearable. Then, just like last time, I get a second wind. I swim and swim until I see a distant shore on the horizon.

Yes!

My lungs begin to work overtime as I kick harder. I slice through the black water like an orca until my feet finally touch the sand—which is when the water and the boat disappear.

———

WE'RE in a familiar clearing in the woods with trees that look like a mix of coral reefs and baobabs. The sky is that of Soma—two counter-rotating cylinders of an O'Neill colony.

A younger Maxwell is sitting on the grass with my mom, who looks to be in her late teens.

"So, Max, what did you want to do?" she asks teasingly.

Max, huh? I guess that's short and sweet. Max doesn't yet have any gray in his hair, and his skin is more bronze than Maxwell's—probably from spending time outside like this.

Seeing my parents together makes my whole body feel tingly and warm—that is, until they begin kissing, much too passionately for my comfort.

Maxwell gapes at them, blinking rapidly.

I clear my throat.

Maxwell rounds on me. "I can't believe I forgot Lidia."

There's a dullness in my chest. "You forgot more than just her."

"Still, you shouldn't have done what you did." He rakes his hands through his hair. "There's got to be a reason I gave up something so wonderful."

"I know what happened," I tell him. "All is not as it seems."

He's not listening, though. He's staring at Mom, his gaze unfocused. She, in the meanwhile, is sucking on the neck of his younger self with an enthusiasm a vampire might envy.

Has my father just recalled being given a major hickey?

"I hope you're right," he says after a moment. "I never want to forget Lidia again."

I sigh. So he was listening. "No hope necessary. I know I'm right."

The memory changes.

SOMETHING I'VE EXPERIENCED in Mom's black window begins to play out.

Three people are in a spacious room, with Mom in a bathtub made of crystal.

Like in Mom's memory, she's pregnant and in the process of birthing me and my twin.

Maxwell's mouth slackens as he stares at his younger self, who's holding Mom's hand like his life depends on it.

"Push, honey." Max kisses the back of Mom's hand. "That's it. I love you."

Maxwell looks at me, his eyes widening beyond what's possible outside the dream world. "I had two daughters!"

I feel a burn behind my eyelids. "You still have them."

His mouth opens and closes, like that of a fish.

"Push!" the midwife orders in the memory.

The crowning baby's head shows up.

Maxwell stares at me unblinkingly.

"You're doing good," says my grandmother in the memory. "Almost there."

The newborn starts screaming.

Maxwell steps toward me, his eyes darting between me and the baby. "Are you...?"

The midwife hands over the gooey newborn to his younger self with a wide grin.

"It's a girl," Max says, his eyes shining with joy. "A baby girl."

The stinging behind my eyes intensifies. "I am."

"Keep pushing!" the midwife orders.

"Which one?" Maxwell asks achingly as the second baby crowns.

"Bailey," I say through the knot in my throat.

"Bailey?" It's as if he's tasting the name.

The second baby screams, and the midwife gives the newborn to my mom.

"Do you know what you're going to call them?" my grandmother asks.

Max gestures at the baby in Mom's arms. "Asha, for my late mother." He looks at the other newborn. "And Bailey, after her grandmother."

With that, Max beams at my namesake-grandmother and lifts baby-me proudly, à la Lion King.

My current-day father finally snaps out of his stupor and closes the distance between us, enveloping me in a hug that's decades overdue.

A tension I've carried since I was a child eases, the hollow ache inside my chest receding. My heart feels full and tingly, expanding until it threatens to burst out of my ribcage.

My father.

I've found him.

Maxwell squeezes me tighter. It's a good thing I don't need to worry about my ribs in the dream world.

In the distance, my grandmother coos at the infants.

"Let me hold one," Mom says hoarsely, and the memory shifts.

———

AN ALL-TOO-FAMILIAR SCENARIO STARTS, playing out a little faster than the prior memories—the beginning of the speedup.

Maxwell, the one I brought with me, wipes away the moisture on his face and shifts his gaze from me to the clearing in the woods where the memory is taking place.

His eyes widen again, and he turns ashen.

My sister and I look to be about seven. We're screaming in terror because our parents are chasing after us with machetes.

"This didn't happen," I tell Maxwell quickly. "You've got to keep that in mind."

But he's already reeling. "No. I was Overtaken. I remember that now." He points at the magma-like fire in the eyes of his younger self.

"Okay, that part happened. But not everything you're about to see did."

He pivots on me, eyes full of old horror and disbelief. "What are you talking about?"

"Do you see those people?" I point at the crowd that's chasing after my parents. "That's Davu and his son, Valerian. You remember what their power is, right?"

Maxwell stills, his jaw working. "Illusions… A lot of people in that crowd are illusionists."

"Stop!" Davu screams at my parents in the memory.

They don't respond, just keep chasing the girls.

Asha trips over a root.

Maxwell reels. "Please, no."

The young me keeps running for a few moments, then looks back, panting. "Asha, no!" she gasps and rushes to her.

Asha is crying.

Little Bailey tries to lift her.

The parents close in.

"This is all an illusion," I say as current-day Maxwell continues to fall apart. "It was meant to fool Phobetor through you."

Max faces the crowd while Mom raises her machete.

"Mommy, no!" the little me screams.

Maxwell clamps his hands over his ears and squeezes his eyes shut, as if that can block the events from playing out in his mind.

The machete whooshes by little Bailey's cheek and slices into Asha's neck.

Blood gushes out of the wound, spraying my young self all over.

Asha's severed head rolls away.

Little Bailey screams.

Maxwell drops to his knees, mumbling something unintelligible as he rocks back and forth.

I reiterate that this is an illusion, but I can't blame him for freaking out. I've experienced this twice now and I know it's fake, yet it still makes me feel nauseated.

Mom's strange eyes gaze at the young me, who's sobbing uncontrollably. Her whole body tenses, her face twisting with alternating expressions of blankness and horror. Then her eyes begin to flicker between the magma fire and her normal brown, and her left hand grabs her right, as if trying to steal the machete from it. Finally, her eyes stay brown, and horror eclipses all else on her face.

"She banished Phobetor," Maxwell mutters, confirming my earlier suspicion. "Same thing happened to me... after I..."

Mom looks at the bloody machete in her hands. Then at headless Asha.

With a raw, guttural moan, she spins around—just as the younger version of my father smashes a fist into her temple.

"Don't do it," Maxwell yells at Max in a hoarse voice.

His younger self doesn't listen. He stalks over to little Bailey and swings the machete.

A primal scream is wrenched from Maxwell's throat.

"It didn't happen," I say as soothingly as I can—though, having never seen this part of the scenario, I'm a little shaken by the fact that he actually went through with it. He killed me.

Phobetor or not, illusion or not, he swung a weapon

at my neck. The neck of my more adorable seven-year-old self. If he were to become Overtaken again, he'd probably kill the grown me in a heartbeat.

Was it too much to wish that parental love would somehow triumph despite all the odds? Did he not love me enough to snap out of it? Did Mom not love Asha enough?

Max's body tenses the way Mom's did, his face also morphing from blankness to horror as his eyes begin to flicker between fiery and amber.

He's beating Phobetor, like she did. Only he, too, has done it when it was too late. Or maybe Phobetor has released them both, thinking that the twins are dead.

That's a scary thought, actually. Could he take over Maxwell again now that he knows I'm alive?

In the memory, Max falls to his knees and screams —which is when the crowd reaches him and Davu knocks him out.

———

THIS NEW MEMORY RUNS FASTER.

Max is hugging his knees, catatonic. He's inside a padded room while Valerian's parents are standing outside, behind a glass door. Whatever they're saying to each other is impossible to hear. If this is the time when Valerian spied on them, they're talking about how my mom has escaped from a similar room, grabbing me along the way.

"I remember being in that cell," Maxwell says, glaring at his younger self.

"Why a cell?" I ask, though I can guess.

"They didn't trust that I'd beaten Phobetor for good," Maxwell says, confirming my suspicion. "I didn't trust myself either."

"But you did beat him, right?" I ask warily. "You're not a ticking bomb?"

His gaze loses focus. "As you've probably guessed, when a dreamwalker is Overtaken, we're fully aware of what Phobetor makes us do. After I did…. what I thought I did, the pain drove me to banish Phobetor from my dream world."

I shift from foot to foot. "Or maybe he just didn't need you enough to push the issue?"

His shoulders slump. "That's also possible, but I doubt it. He's been trying to get back in. In fact, it's been a battle to keep him out all these years—a battle I've gotten better at with time. But you're right. There are no guarantees. It might be wise to always keep a careful eye on me."

That's exactly what I plan to do, but there's no reason to belabor it. Instead, I say, "He's back in Mom's dreams."

Maxwell lifts a shaky hand to his forehead. "Of course. That was Lidia in a coma. How could I have forgotten about that?"

I pat his shoulder. "It's a lot to take in."

"So Phobetor has her?"

"I'm not sure," I say and explain what happened in

the subdream.

Maxwell frowns. "That doesn't prove he took her over. In fact, if she never goes into REM sleep, he'll have a hard time making her an Overtaken. I think he just took advantage of an opportunity. Bailey..." He looks at me pleadingly. "Promise me you won't go back into Lidia's dreams."

"But the coma—"

"Let me think on that." He shifts his attention to his unmoving younger self.

Davu opens a small window. "Are you hungry?"

Max doesn't reply.

"I remember this," Maxwell says. "It was a month before I escaped."

Before I can ask how he escaped, or anything else, the memory changes.

———

THINGS SPEED UP EVEN MORE.

We're in a large meeting room. A dozen people are sitting in a circle, Valerian's and my parents among them. In the middle of the circle is Nostradamus and his werewolf.

I happen to know kid Valerian is here too, but he's hiding using his powers, so he's not part of my father's memories.

"The prophecy," Maxwell says darkly. "That cursed thing cost me everything."

Nostradamus begins to speak. "If Phobetor isn't

stopped, he'll destroy everyone, not just your little world."

"We know this," Max says. "Tell us something we don't."

"There's one thing that will give you a chance at victory," Nostradamus says. "A minuscule chance."

Mom looks at the seer skeptically. "What is it?"

"Only Two working as One can defeat the god of nightmares," Nostradamus says. "Remember, only Two working as One."

Everyone gazes at him in confusion.

"That's much too vague," my mom says. "Who are the Two? How do you work as One?"

Nostradamus stands up. "I might've already said too much."

Everybody starts shouting questions, but the werewolf growls at them and leads the seer out of the room.

———

THIS MEMORY LOOKS like a movie on fast-forward.

Mom and Max are watching Asha and me play in the distance.

Maxwell gazes longingly in the same direction.

"Two working as One doesn't have to mean the twins," Mom says, sounding like a chipmunk. "You and I are soulmates—that's a type of two working as one, isn't it?"

"You can make that argument, true," Max says, also

sounding funny due to the speedup. "But let's be honest with ourselves. Without ever having heard of the seer, the girls play a game they call 'two as one.' Are we to ignore that?"

Mom twists a ring on her finger. "That game could be a coincidence. Even if it's not, are we really going to allow our children to fight Phobetor?"

Max squeezes her hand. "That's a different conversation altogether. Whether or not us being soulmates means we're Two as One, I'd rather defeat Phobetor myself than have my daughters be forced to do it."

She nods. "Everyone says we're the most powerful dreamwalkers they know. The girls don't seem to be stronger. At least, not yet."

"I guess that's that," Max says. "We're going to tell everyone that we're certain the prophecy is about us."

Mom squares her shoulders. "We're going to battle Phobetor."

———

IN THE NEXT MEMORY, Max is a young child. He's playing a game with other boys, the details of which are hard to make out due to the speedup.

The memory that comes after this takes place in the padded room again, only this time Max isn't catatonic. He stares intently at the corner of the room. Thanks to the speedup, what must've taken a long time for him happens almost in an eyeblink.

A shining plasma gate opens in the corner of the room. It looks like the gates at the hubs, only smaller and fainter.

A woman steps out of the gate. "You have only two favors left. Use this one wisely."

In lieu of an answer, Max leaps into the gate.

Before I can ask Maxwell pertinent questions about his unusual form of escape, the next memory starts. In it, my parents are battling in the dream world—at least I assume that's where they are, since when Mom punches a wall behind Max, it shatters into pieces.

"Training for the big battle," Maxwell says without being prompted.

I guess he doesn't want me to think he beat his wife.

When I refocus on the memories, Max is at a funeral, and the memory after that looks like my parents' wedding.

Now things begin to move so fast I can only guess at what I see. It seems like the next memory is that of a battle happening in a subdream-like space. I get a glimpse of Phobetor, as well as Mom and Max.

The next thing I catch is the end of the battle. Both my parents have fiery eyes.

What follows flashes by so fast it's impossible to make out, and then the world explodes around us, jolting me awake.

CHAPTER THIRTEEN

I OPEN my eyes in the waking world.

Virgil looks at me curiously as I lean back in the wheelchair to catch my breath.

That was a lot of information all at once. It's a good thing I'd sat down before I started, as my legs are actually feeling weak.

Maxwell sits up on the gurney. He looks at his empty palms, then touches his fingers to his lips while looking at me as if for the first time.

"Do you remember now?" I ask cautiously.

"I remember everything." His voice is choked with emotion.

For a few moments, we just stare at each other. Then Virgil coughs theatrically.

I have no idea what the vampire thinks is going on here, but I don't care. I stand up as Maxwell slides his legs down the gurney.

As soon as he's off the bed, he envelops me in a fierce hug.

My heart flutters even more rapidly here in the real world. My father's scent, clean and woodsy, tugs at something in the back of my mind, evoking a feeling of comfort and safety. My usual germ fears are far from my mind, and even after we pull apart, I don't feel the slightest urge to hygieia.

"Your mother," Maxwell says raggedly. "Can you please take me to her?"

I glance at Virgil, who's watching us with a puzzled frown. Catching my gaze, he nods and leads us out.

I use the time as we walk to compose myself. Just because my father now remembers me doesn't mean all our problems are solved.

When we get to Mom's room, the two gnomes are still chatting. Ignoring them and Virgil, Maxwell rushes to Mom's tricked-out bed and stares at her greedily, eyes gleaming with moisture.

"Open it," he says. "Please."

Dr. Xipil pauses his animated discussion with Itzel, touches the remote, and the clamshell glass opens up. He and Itzel then tactfully step away, while Maxwell grabs Mom's hand and closes his eyes.

"Are you going into her dreams?" I ask softly, coming up to stand next to him.

He shakes his head. "I'm no use to anyone if Phobetor takes me over again. Or makes me go insane."

I lay my hand over his palm, which is still squeezing my mom's hand. "How do we save her then?"

He looks at me. "We need to go to Soma to reunite with Asha."

I gape at him, struck speechless.

I'm still wrapping my mind around finding my father. To also gain a sister? My twin? I can't even—

"Once you and Asha meet, you'll have to decide if you're willing to follow the prophecy," Maxwell says, and his words hit me like a bucket of crushed ice. "Once Phobetor is defeated, any of us can go into your mother's dreams, give her back her past, and jolt her awake."

Phobetor defeated.

Prophecy.

Until this moment, these were merely abstract concepts.

Now I have no choice but to consider them, even though my brain refuses to compute it all.

"I don't know about my sister, but I'm not a hero from some fairy tale," I say slowly. "Even if I were, how would I defeat a god?"

"By, among other things, believing in yourself," Maxwell says solemnly.

Pom's fur turns pitch black on my wrist. "Sure. Why didn't you say so before? I'll just believe in myself all the way to a miracle. Maybe I'll turn lead into gold while I'm at it."

My father shakes his head. "Even before Nostradamus, our people believed we would have to deal with Phobetor one day. Believed that he *could* be defeated."

I take a step back. "I saw him close up."

"And he had me under his power," Maxwell says softly. "I understand the magnitude of this task better than anyone."

I begin to pace the room.

Can I do this?

No clue. Probably not, though. My parents tried, and that didn't work out so well for them. It would be a shame to find my twin, just to have Phobetor Overtake us and have us kill each other.

Still, going to Soma and meeting my sister is the first step in this insane plan, and it's something I'd want to do even if Phobetor didn't exist. Once there, if there's no other way to wake Mom, and if Asha's on board, we can revisit the whole battling Phobetor idea.

Who knows? I may not be a hero, but if I train a bit, maybe I could at least bluff Phobetor into letting me into Mom's dream world. I did manage to jolt away from him the last time. That's something.

I stop pacing and face my father. "Let's do it. Take me to Soma."

CHAPTER FOURTEEN

MAXWELL SMILES PROUDLY. "That's my girl."

I'm not sure how to respond to that—or to the warm glow his words generate in my chest—but I don't have to because Valerian walks into the room.

His gaze falls on Maxwell's face, and his eyes widen. "Max? Max Spidi?"

Spidi? Is that my real last name? It makes sense that Mom would take on our current one—Spade—as a way to stay more incognito in her exile.

Maxwell's jaw hangs open. "Valerian? Valerian Bale?"

Aha. Seems like between their black windows and the masks we were all wearing on our journey to Necronia, neither my father nor Valerian had realized they knew each other.

That's good. If I'd found out that Valerian knew about my father and didn't tell me, I'd have trouble forgiving that kind of betrayal.

Valerian's stunned gaze shifts back and forth between us. "Does Bailey know that you're her—"

"Father? Yes," Maxwell says.

"Her father?" Itzel exclaims, finally tearing herself away from her conversation with Dr. Xipil.

Speaking over each other, Maxwell and I explain our recent revelation. As we speak, the puzzled look on Virgil's face transforms into one of understanding and relief.

I don't know what he thought when Maxwell and I were hugging, but I wouldn't be surprised if he was worried about having an even more "uncomfortable" conversation with Valerian.

When the explanations are over, I take Valerian aside. "What took you so long?"

He rakes his fingers through his dark, thick hair. "I had to make sure everyone was all right, then clean up a huge mess you made at my VR company."

Puck. With all the family drama, I'd forgotten about the people who got knocked out on the skyscraper roof hub. "How's everyone?"

"The members of the New York Council woke up and are as good as new," he says. "More measures will be taken when they sleep now, so even if Collywobbles wants to bribe anyone else into releasing them, they'll have a devil of a time dealing with all the security precautions."

I nod approvingly. "What about Felix and Ariel?"

"Never better. I also got the ball rolling to get Rowan settled on Earth—which wasn't an easy conversation. Finally, I made sure Dylan has a lab and financing to do any research she wants."

"Fine," I say with mock grumpiness. "I guess you didn't completely waste the hours I gave you. Now what is that mess you claim I made? Is the video game I'm starring in selling poorly?"

Valerian's face darkens. "The game is fine, but Rattie was sleeping in one of our office's napping units when he attacked you."

Ah, right. I myself slept in one of those once—which is when I'd actually made a dream link to Rattie. I bet he'd done the same with me around the same time; that's how he was able to attack me.

Then Valerian's meaning dawns on me.

Rattie's attack. I killed him, a dreamwalker, during a dreamwalk. That means—

"He went homicidally insane," Valerian says grimly, confirming my suspicion. "The security footage was brutal. He slaughtered everyone on his way out of the office building, and some pedestrians after that."

Bile rises in my throat. "Anyone I know?"

"I'm not sure who you know at the company," Valerian says and rattles out a bunch of names that don't sound familiar.

"What about Bernard?" I ask. Having dreamwalked in the man and nudged him to reunite with his estranged daughter, I feel invested in his fate.

"He was one of the lucky ones," Valerian says. "He had plans with his daughter that evening."

Whew. That's something. Still, I can't help but feel

awful—especially since I hadn't given the consequences of defeating Rattie a single thought. Then again, I was too busy dying of the virus shortly after that battle, and then dealing with a score of Overtaken attacks and a family reunion.

Swallowing the lump in my throat, I ask, "Where's Rattie now?"

Valerian frowns. "No one knows, and not for a lack of trying. He took a cab to JFK without killing the driver. Felix helped us get the airport security footage, and we saw Rattie heading toward the hub. His eyes were those of an Overtaken. The theory is that he fell asleep after his murder spree, and Collywobbles took over his body."

"What's a Collywobbles?" Maxwell asks, approaching us.

"That's what we call the god of nightmares," I explain. "Valerian believes that calling him by his real name gives him more power."

Valerian takes my hand and rubs my palm with his thumb. "Not a lot of power, mind you, but why give him any? Also, I kind of like the idea of using a disrespectful nickname for him. I bet it would infuriate him if he knew."

Maxwell glances at our joined hands, a faint smile touching the corners of his eyes. "We always knew the two of you would end up together. That you found each other in exile is extraordinary."

Are we together? I guess it's close enough. I

contentedly squeeze Valerian's hand. "Don't forget we also did it without any memories of our past. It boggles the mind if you think about it."

The look Valerian gives me makes something inside me melt into a gooey puddle.

"It's very romantic," Itzel says, coming up to us with Dr. Xipil—whom she looks at meaningfully for some reason.

At the mention of romance, my father's gaze falls on Mom's contraption, and his expression turns somber. "We need to talk." He gives the gnomes and Virgil a hard look. "In private."

Itzel and Dr. Xipil nod and step out of the room.

Virgil doesn't.

"Go," Valerian orders, jabbing his thumb at the door.

Virgil exits with visible reluctance.

"Don't bother eavesdropping," Valerian says as the vampire begins to close the door behind himself. "I'm going to be using my powers to shield us."

"Fine," Virgil says over his shoulder. "If Maxwell or Bailey attack you, don't come crying to me after."

Before Valerian can answer, the vampire is gone.

Valerian looks at Maxwell. "This is about going to Soma, isn't it?"

Maxwell nods solemnly.

"I've been thinking along the same lines," Valerian says. "But it's impossible to get there."

My heart sinks. "Why?"

"The trip from here to Soma goes through extremely dangerous Otherlands," Valerian says.

"Mom and I must've made the journey once," I say. "And you did too."

"That was before all the Otherlands started teeming with the Overtaken," he says. "If we were to try to go to Soma now, our trip from Necronia would seem like a leisurely stroll in comparison."

The sinking sensation intensifies. "What if we brought an army of vampires with us?"

Valerian shakes his head. "Still too dangerous. Also, we're trying to keep the location of Soma a secret."

Maxwell nods. "Soma's very existence must stay a secret."

I look at him. "How can a world's existence ever be a secret? Isn't there a hub that some Cognizant could accidentally stumble onto?"

"Soma is special," Maxwell says. "There's only a single gate leading to and from it. The entry gate for Soma is hidden on a nondescript world, far from the regular hub."

"So that's it?" I don't bother hiding the disappointment in my voice. "I don't get to meet my twin?"

"I'm sorry," Valerian says, and looks it.

"There is a way," Maxwell says. "Otherwise, why would I suggest we go to Soma?"

I belatedly recall a memory of his. "Of course. You want to use that woman who sprung you from Soma."

"She owes me one last favor," Maxwell says. "And

I'm glad I didn't use up that favor when I was sick with the virus. I suspected I might have to return to Soma one day."

Wow. Talk about self-discipline. When I had that virus, I would've called in every favor and spent every penny to get closer to the cure.

"What are you two talking about?" Valerian asks.

"A teleporter," Maxwell says. "A world jumper at that."

I wanted to ask him about that when I first saw the memory, but things moved too fast, so I didn't get a chance. Teleporters are among the rarest Cognizant types, and the most powerful of them—a tiny minority of an already small group—are world jumpers. It is said that world jumpers can create personal gates to Otherlands.

Personally, I've never met any of them. If it weren't for the hubs, I would doubt that world jumpers exist. Legends say the gates in the hubs were created by a mix of gnome technology and a group of ultra-powerful world jumpers, sometimes called the gate makers.

"I thought world jumpers were a myth," Valerian says, echoing my thoughts.

"They're real," Maxwell says. "They prefer to live on worlds that don't have hubs—because they can. So, naturally, they're hard for the rest of us to come across. The jumper who owes me needed a dreamwalker, so she found me, not the other way around."

Valerian frowns. "But if she's on another world, and without a hub, how are we going to recruit her?"

"Dreamwalking isn't constrained by Otherland boundaries," Maxwell says. "If it were, Phobetor wouldn't be as big a problem as he is."

"Call him Collywobbles," Valerian says, almost on autopilot. "Do you think your world jumper is sleeping right now?"

"There's only one way to find out." Maxwell looks at me. "Can you put me in REM sleep?"

"You don't need me to put you to sleep to get to the dream world." I wave my wristband as its fur turns brown. "You can use Pom instead."

"What's a pom?" Maxwell asks, then looks at my pet, eyes widening. "Oh, wow. That's a creature, and it's in REM sleep."

"*He* is," I say, and explain that Pom is a looft, a symbiotic creature that lives on moofts.

Maxwell takes a half step back. "How did you get him in the first place? Dream world access is nice, but to willingly let a parasite leech your—"

"He's a symbiont." The defensiveness in my voice is ironic, given how much I've teased Pom about this very thing.

"I was wondering about this too." Valerian looks at Pom. "How did the two of you end up together?"

Smiling, I pet Pom's fur. "A patient of mine was badgering me to go to the South Gomorran Petting Zoo. She said it was the most soothing experience she's ever encountered, and that I could use it as dream therapy. I eventually gave in." I look at Valerian to make sure he appreciates what a great sacrifice that was for someone as wary of germs as I am. "According to my extensive research, moofts were the only creatures at that zoo that were never featured in an article about cross-species transmission of disease. So at the urging of my patient, I reached out to touch one. My hand landed on the most colorful and furry section of the creature—which turned out to have been a budding looft. The looft got attached to my wrist. Naturally, I freaked out at first. But then I learned about loofts and that they spend the majority of their lives in REM sleep, so I realized the potential. Long story short, I met Pom in the dream world, fell in love with his cuteness, and now he's my best friend."

A best friend who recently admitted to using a section of my brain, but still. What's a few neurons among friends? I was probably too smart for my own good.

Maxwell wrinkles his nose. "If you don't mind, I'd rather just go into REM sleep from my own dreams."

Huh. Is my father wary of touching Pom for the same reason I'd be—a totally reasonable and rational fear of viruses and bacteria that everyone else in the world lacks for unfathomable-to-me reasons?

Nah. He'd hugged me without a second thought.

Then again, I'd also hugged him without hesitation.

"Lie down on the floor," I say, figuring if he's really like me, he'll object to that unsanitary instruction.

He lies down. He either doesn't share my qualms or

the prospect of touching Pom was the worse evil. "I'm ready."

Figuring this might be a good time to practice using my sleep-inducing power remotely, I try it out.

It works. My father is instantly in REM sleep.

Seizing the moment, I turn to Valerian. "Did you miss me?"

His ocean-blue eyes glimmer. "What do you think?"

The room around us shimmers and becomes a lush bedroom once more, the one with an enormous bed swathed in silk sheets and scattered with rose petals.

I swallow hard, my pulse picking up. "I think you couldn't stop thinking about me."

He closes the distance between us and brushes his fingers along my jaw. His touch sends an electrical jolt through my body, making my skin prickle and my breathing hitch in my throat.

Biting my lip, I reach out to squeeze his muscular forearm. "Am I touching the real you?"

He nods, his eyes falling to my mouth.

Without a second thought, I rise on tiptoe and kiss him.

He returns the kiss hungrily, his tongue sweeping over the closed seam of my lips—which part of their own accord. He immediately takes advantage, deepening the kiss, and my mind goes pleasantly blank, empty of thoughts about germs or nearby parents or anything else. All I am is blissful awareness of how soft his lips are, how—

He picks me up and strides toward the bed.

Wow. Some of this can't be real.

"You think you can handle more?" His voice is like heated molasses.

I nod as our eyes meet, my racing pulse making it difficult to speak.

His clothes disappear, and I no longer care if this is real or not. Pom's fur turns coral pink on my wrist, and my own clothes feel like a straitjacket as heat thrums under my skin, making me feel like I'm melting. Breathing raggedly, I reach out to stroke the smooth, hard muscles of his chest and—

Valerian curses, and his clothes reappear as the bedroom poofs out of existence, revealing the reason.

Maxwell has just sat up.

Puck. Did he have to finish his dreamwalking so quickly?

I fight the urge to fan myself. How embarrassing would it be if I asked Valerian to use his powers to give me a cold shower?

"Later," Valerian promises in a soft whisper, and I nod, flushing.

"It's a date," I whisper back. "And when it happens, I don't want any illusions. Not the first time."

Valerian's eyes darken. "Your wish is my command."

"It's done," Maxwell says, scrubbing a hand over his face. "We have a few minutes before she arrives."

I look around the room, forcing myself to focus on something other than Valerian. "We're taking Mom with us, right?"

"Of course," Maxwell says.

"And leaving as soon as the jumper shows up?"

He nods. "Why wait?"

"In that case, we need the remote for Mom's bed."

Valerian's already on it. "I'll go talk to Dr. Xipil and tell Virgil we're leaving."

"But don't tell them where we're going," Maxwell says.

Valerian opens the door. "I'm not the one who blabbed about Soma's location to a random teleporter."

My father stiffens. "I didn't have a choice."

"Well, I do, and I don't intend to say anything." Not waiting for a reply, Valerian walks out.

Maxwell turns to me. "He's different than I remember him. Tougher. More like his father."

"What about me?" I ask. "Am I different?"

"I don't know yet." He smiles. "Ask me again once we get to know each other a little better."

I grin back at him. "Deal."

"Actually, would you mind telling me something about yourself?" he asks. "You mentioned patients earlier. Are you a doctor?"

I tell him about the dream therapy I pioneered, and as I do, I can see his shoulders straighten with pride.

"Is that your main passion?" he asks after I'm done.

"There's also virtual reality games," I say. "I hope to use that technology to create something similar to dream therapy, but more accessible."

He smiles. "You're a lot like your namesake grandmother. She, too, is a healer in her heart of hearts."

"I can't wait to meet her," I say, then frown. "She's alive, right? She was already old in your memories, and Valerian said that time flows faster on Soma."

"Dreamwalkers live very long lives," Maxwell says. "Barring some unfortunate accident, Mama B should be alive, and in good health."

"How long is long?" I ask. This is something I've always wondered but couldn't ask Mom, who disliked any topic having to do with our powers. "Is it centuries, like ubers, or—"

"That's about right. And before you ask, so do illusionists." He gives me a wink.

I try my best not to flush again. How much did he hear and see of my makeout session with Valerian? "How about you tell me about your life in exile?" I ask, both to change the topic and because I'm genuinely curious.

For all I know, I might have a stepmom—or half-siblings.

My father sighs. "There isn't much to tell. For a while, I abandoned dreamwalking completely and became a musician."

Huh. That's random. "Which instruments did you play?"

"Whichever I could get my hands on. Eventually, I became a conductor. I'm still famous on the world I exiled myself to."

I bite my lip. "Were you lonely?"

"I didn't remarry, if that's what you mean." He looks down. "I didn't remember you and Lidia, but on some level, I think I knew something. It's hard to explain. The very thought of starting a family was abhorrent."

Mom didn't date either. Her life was pretty miserable, in fact. I hope I brought her some happiness, but he didn't have even that much.

"I'm sorry," I say.

He looks up. "Don't feel sorry for me. I channeled all those pent-up emotions into my music. In a real way, a lot of people got joy from that pain, and I'm okay with that."

The door opens again, and Valerian walks in. "All set." He hands Maxwell the remote for Mom's bed.

Maxwell presses a button, and the clamshell closes. "Do we need to change some nutrition bag or anything like that?"

"I have all the instructions," Valerian says. "This is something we'll be able to do easily on Soma."

My father inclines his head. "Thank you so much, Valerian. Davu would be so very proud."

Eyes gleaming, Valerian mumbles a thanks.

A shining plasma gate suddenly opens in the corner of the room. It looks like the one from Maxwell's memory—similar to the ones at the hubs but smaller and not as bright.

The woman from the memory steps out of the gate. Her face is classically beautiful, and her highly intelligent eyes dart around the room worriedly until she catches sight of Maxwell.

Relaxing, she makes the gate she came from

disappear, and two more gates show up, one on each side of her.

"This is your last favor," she says to Maxwell, her voice more melodic now that it's not sped up.

"Thanks, Karina," Maxwell says. "You might've just saved the Cogniverse."

"Sure," Karina says with a heavy dose of skepticism. "Just remember, regardless of how the world saving goes, we're through. If I see you in my dreams again, my next gate will open under your feet, and it will exit above an erupting volcano. On a world with no oxygen."

Before anyone can comment on her threat, she steps into one of the gates, and the gate shimmers out of existence.

Well, okay then. That's one way to have the last word.

"We must hurry," Maxwell says and fiddles with the controls on Mom's bed.

"Can we trust this Karina?" I ask. "What if she's done the whole top-of-volcano gate preemptively?"

Maxwell smiles. "Karina is a woman of her word. This gate leads to Soma. And if I do visit her dreams again, a gate will indeed open under my feet and plunge me into a volcano, on a world without oxygen." On that cheerful note, he rolls Mom's bed into the gate and steps through himself.

"Your father has always been a good judge of character," Valerian says, and before I can reply, he also enters the gate.

I take a breath and glance down at my wrist, where Pom's fur is turning black.

Here goes nothing.

Volcano, here I come.

CHAPTER FIFTEEN

I STEP out into a padded glass room, where there's definitely oxygen.

I recognize it immediately, and judging by Maxwell and Valerian's faces, they must as well.

This is where my father was being held when he escaped with Karina's help.

Maxwell curses. "I should've been more careful. One of Karina's least endearing qualities is her sense of humor. I asked her to bring me back to Soma. I bet she thought it would be funny to bring me back exactly where she'd sprung me from."

Valerian knocks on the glass. "Feels bulletproof."

Maxwell yells out loud.

Since there's no one around, no one answers.

I scan the corners where the walls meet the ceiling until I hit jackpot—a gizmo that could be a camera.

I wave at the hopefully-camera like a maniac.

Nothing happens.

Valerian examines the door lock and curses in frustration.

We wait.

Valerian starts to pace.

No one comes.

"If Lidia were awake, she might know how to beat that lock," Maxwell says. "She was good with such things."

"If Mom were awake, we might not even be here," I mutter.

Maxwell slides down a soft wall until he's sitting on the floor in a pose that reminds me of when he was locked in this room in his memory. "No one knows we're here. We could starve."

"I wouldn't worry about that," I say. "We'll die of thirst long before that."

Valerian casts a furtive glance at Mom's bed.

"We're not stealing Mom's nutrients, if that's what you're thinking," I tell him sternly. "And if it is what you're thinking, shame on you."

Valerian folds his arms across his chest. "I fleetingly considered using the contraption as a battering ram but instantly dismissed the idea."

I pinch the bridge of my nose. "That's even worse than stealing her food."

"Well, I wasn't going to steal her food in the first place," he says.

"Children," Maxwell mutters. "Focus on workable solutions. Please."

Stroking Pom's fur to calm myself, I thoughtfully

study my father. "You're from here. You must have dream connections with someone. Why don't you dreamwalk in a local and ask them for help?"

Maxwell theatrically smacks himself on the forehead. "How did I not think of that? My only excuse is that I've only recently remembered that I know people who live here."

I scratch my chin. "I hadn't thought of that before. Who did you think they were when you saw them in your tower of sleepers? I bet even *I* was there…"

"What's a tower of sleepers?" Maxwell asks.

As I explain, a slow smile spreads over his face. "What you call a tower of sleepers is just your own personal dream construct to deal with the problem of dreamwalking in someone you've made a connection with. Mine is just a room with paintings of the people whose dreams I'd like to visit."

"I use paintings too," I say. "But for my memory gallery, which is a way to revisit the memories I like."

"There you go," Maxwell says. "But to answer your original question, if you don't remember someone, they won't appear as a dream contact, regardless of how you represent such things in your dream world. It's not like a phone that has a list of contacts stored in its memory. Dream constructs use your mind—so if you forget a person, they won't appear in your tower of sleepers."

"That makes sense," I say. "Mom must've had a dream connection with both me and Asha, but I bet that after her exile, she never saw the two of us in her version of the tower of sleepers, only me."

"All that is fascinating," Valerian says. "But could you shelve dreamwalk theory until after we're freed?"

Maxwell stretches out on the floor. "Put me in REM sleep."

I do, and Valerian and I both pace as we wait.

After what feels like many hours, my father sits up. "I just spoke with your grandmother. Help should be on the way."

My grandmother.

I'm about to see her.

The idea makes me breathless—that or we're running out of oxygen in this room.

After what feels like a few more hours, a man walks up to the glass. Wearing a helmet and a chrome bodysuit, he looks like he's stepped off a set of a show about deep space exploration. He even holds what looks like a space gun—a long, sleek rifle-like thing.

Valerian makes LEGO letters appear in my line of vision: *That's one of the guards. Most of them are illusionists and therefore don't usually need to use weapons. Do you have any idea why your grandmother would send one to escort us out like this?*

I shrug, as does Maxwell—who must've seen the same question.

"Stay away from the door," the guard says.

As we back away, Maxwell explains about Mom's bed.

The guard unlocks the door and orders us to walk in front of him in the direction he says.

We oblige, with my father controlling the bed to make it ride ahead of us.

As we walk, I can't help but notice something I didn't realize when experiencing other people's memories of Soma. The surroundings have a definite spaceship vibe. I don't know if it's the silvery walls that lack any decorations or the very basic furniture and the guard's uniform.

When we exit the structure with the "jail," the spaceship feel grows stronger. The buildings around us are silvery and overly geometric in their shape—like someone had printed them out in one shot instead of building them with metal and cement, the way it's done on Gomorrah and Earth.

Spotting Valerian looking up at the sky, I follow his gaze.

How cool. Though I've seen this sky arrangement in the memories, looking at it live is that much more surreal. The road we're currently walking on seems to lead into the sky that looks like a circle. To the side of us, the ground seems to slope up, with forests and more buildings above our heads.

"So trippy," I breathe, my neck aching from the strain of looking up at such a steep angle. "I avoid these types of environments in the dream world because they seem too unrealistic."

"That's one of the reasons we need illusionists on Soma," Maxwell says, taking on a professorial tone that reminds me of Dylan. "Soma founders expected people to go crazy from staring at the weird sky. Illusionists can make it all look normal."

As if to illustrate the point, Valerian uses his powers to unfold the environment around us, making the sky look all-encompassing, as usual. The houses that were in the sky show up as distant structures on the horizon.

"Don't." I touch his elbow. "I'm not stir crazy yet."

The surreal reality comes back.

I gape at everything until we walk into a cuboid structure, where the guard leads us into what looks like a cafeteria. There are shiny metal tables and chairs all around, but only one of them is occupied.

It's an older woman with white curly hair, and I recognize her immediately.

It's Bailey, my grandmother.

CHAPTER SIXTEEN

DROPPING something that looks like a toothpaste tube onto a silvery tray, my grandmother leaps to her feet and rushes over to Mom's bed. Lips trembling, she stares down for a long minute as I watch her, my chest heavy.

Somberly, my father opens the clamshell-like top of the contraption, and my grandmother bends over her daughter and kisses her gently on the forehead.

I can't even imagine what she must be feeling.

When she looks up at my father, her eyes are swimming with tears. "It's as you said. Not even a hint of sleep. My poor Lia."

Lia? I've never heard anyone call Mom that. I like it, though.

Blinking a few times, my grandmother straightens her spine and turns to the guard. "Please take Lia's bed to the medical bay."

The guard glances at us uneasily. "They haven't been cleared."

"Leave me the gun then," she snaps.

The guard walks over and hands her the gun, which she accepts with obvious distaste.

My father gives the guard the remote for Mom's bed and explains how to use it. Reluctantly, the guard makes Mom's bed roll out and follows behind it.

My grandmother stares after them with visible longing. When the guard is completely out of sight, she composes herself and turns to Valerian. "You've grown to be a fine young man," she says, her voice softening to a kind, motherly tone. "Can you be a dear and make sure no one can overhear us?"

Looking a little taken aback, Valerian nods and presumably does as she asks, while my grandmother turns her razor-sharp gaze on me.

"Come, child. Let me take a look at you."

I take a reluctant step in her direction.

Will she hug me or shoot me with that gun?

Her gray eyes—identical to mine—moisten again as they scan me from head to foot. "You're so much like your sister," she says softly. "Yet so unlike her at the same time."

"You have some of Mom's features," I say with a shy smile. "And mine."

Laugh lines appear at the corners of her eyes. "Are you sure it's not the two of you who have my features, little bee?"

Was that my nickname? If so, I don't remember it at all.

"Where's Asha?" Maxwell asks.

"All in good time," my grandmother says, her face smoothing out. "You'll have to forgive me for the security measures. We've had the Overtaken try to sneak into the gate." Her hand tightens on the gun.

Valerian's expression darkens. "Overtaken here, on Soma?"

"I'm afraid so. And not just from the Otherlands either. Some Soma citizens have been succumbing. That's why the guards now walk around armed at all times."

"But how?" I ask. "Is anyone dumb enough to listen to other people's description of nightmares?"

She shakes her head. "Phobetor's power has now grown to the point where he can work his vileness through a regular nightmare, especially if the sleeper's guard happens to be down."

"Call him Collywobbles," Valerian says, and explains why.

"That's like trying to stop an ocean with a dam, but I'll do as you ask," she says. "Now, please, let's get the unpleasantness taken care of. Lie down." She gestures at the nearby benches.

Valerian pulls out a hygieia device and waves it over a bench for me.

I lie down, and he does the same.

My grandmother points a hand at Valerian and his body slumps. She does the same to my father next.

I feel them both in REM sleep and realize how the clearing works. If we've been Overtaken, dreamwalking in us will reveal it.

She points a hand at me, and I instantly fall asleep.

———

VALERIAN AND I are in his bed, making out. Suddenly, he disappears and I find myself clothed and standing in a cafeteria-like room.

My wrist is lacking Pom. This, combined with the sight of prone Maxwell and Valerian, informs me of two things: I'm asleep, and my grandmother is dreamwalking in me at the moment.

Probably.

"Where are you?" I ask, looking around.

With a satisfied chuckle, she drops her invisibility. Here, in the dream world, she looks to be about my age, and our resemblance is even more noticeable.

"So, you and Valerian," she says with a mischievous grin. "Unless that dream was more along the lines of wishful thinking?"

I flush. "It's in the early stages. Let's not jinx it by talking about it, okay?"

"Sure thing. For what it's worth, his dream of you leaves me little doubt about his feelings." She winks.

My blush intensifies, and I do my best to change the subject. "You've cleared Valerian, right?"

"And you," she says.

I jerk my chin at Maxwell. "What about him?"

Her expression turns more somber. "He's keeping the beast at bay. I will look out for him."

I'm glad she's spared me from having to suggest the same thing.

With his best Cheshire Cat impersonation to date, Pom appears on my shoulder.

"Hello, Bailey's Grandmother," he says, his fur morphing from light orange to teal. "It's nice to meet you. I'm Pom."

Her eyes grow cartoonishly wide. "That's not a dream construct, is it?"

"I'm not," he says.

"He's my best friend," I say, and explain about my symbiotic relationship with the looft.

"Well, now I've seen everything," she says, shaking her head in amazement. "It's a pleasure to meet you, Pom."

He turns a deep purple. "The pleasure is mine."

"Now, if you don't mind, I want to catch up with my grandchild."

"Of course, Grandmother," Pom says.

"Call me Mama B," she replies with a grin. "Everyone else does."

"Later, Mama B," Pom chirps and disappears—but his paws are still digging into my shoulder, so I know he's just turned invisible.

"He's a charmer," she says.

"That he is."

She makes the room around us change to a forest meadow, gracefully sinks onto the grass, and pats a place next to her.

Since we're in a dream and therefore without germs, I sit.

"Tell me a little bit about yourself," she says. "Where do you and Lia live?"

I tell her about Gomorrah, my job, and my recent misadventures, but I don't go too much into Mom's troubles before the coma.

"What about you?" I ask when I'm done. "Tell me what your life has been like."

"In a word, busy," she says with a sigh. "My typical day consists of running around Soma like a madwoman. I don't spend nearly as much time with my great-grandchild as—"

"Wait." I stare at her openmouthed. "My sister is—"

"Married and has a daughter." She makes two people appear in front of me, an attractive, strong-featured man who looks familiar and a girl about eight years old.

I peer at the man, picturing him without his dark, neatly groomed beard. "That's Kojo, isn't it?" I say, remembering the name of another one of our childhood friends.

"It is, and the name of that precious one is Chloe," she says with great-grandmotherly pride. She grins at me. "You're an aunt."

I look Dream Chloe over. With that mischievous smile and the halo of curls that make her look like a dark-headed dandelion, she might just be cuter than Pom. "Where is she? Out there, in the real world, I mean? And where's Asha?"

I'm dying to meet my twin.

My grandmother sighs. "I think we'd better wake up so I fill you in along with everyone else."

Huh, okay. I wonder what the mystery's all about. "Before we go, do you want me to call you Mama B or Grandmother or—"

She beams at me. "When you and Asha were small, you called me Bebe."

"Bebe it is," I say and jolt myself awake.

———

FEELING GROGGY, I get up from the bench, and my father and Valerian do the same.

Bebe walks over to a nearby machine and presses a couple of buttons. The machine dispenses three silver cubes, and she sets them on the table near her tray. "Might as well eat while we talk."

"Eat?" I examine the cubes for any sign of edibleness.

She unfolds one cube until it becomes a tray like hers, with clear tubes of some gray substance inside. She squirts the paste-like stuff into her mouth and swallows. "These will serve every nutritional need."

"And they're sterile," Valerian says reassuringly. Under his breath, he adds, "Perhaps too much so."

I take a seat and squirt a tube into my mouth, half expecting the minty flavor of toothpaste.

Nope. There's no taste. I've never eaten something this neutral before. There's no flavor whatsoever, and even the texture of the substance is bland.

Oh, well. I don't care as long as it's really sterile. The last thing I want is to come all this way just to die of salmonella poisoning before I even meet my twin.

Bebe looks at Valerian. "Can you be a dear and use your powers to make me think I'm eating something more palatable?"

He nods, and the next time she squirts the goo into her mouth, she looks a lot happier.

"I didn't realize your kind could create the illusion of taste," I say.

"Of course," Valerian replies. "If we couldn't, you'd be able to use the sense of taste to know you're being fooled."

That makes sense. When I kissed an illusory version of him, I couldn't tell the difference. Taste was involved.

Oops. Pom is turning coral pink on my wrist.

I wave my tube at Valerian. "Can you make mine taste like manna?"

"I can do better." He rummages in his pocket and hands me a familiar manna packet. "I picked up some before we left."

I beam at him. "Thank you." As I take the gift, my fingers brush his skin, and Pom's coral-pink color deepens.

Bebe and my father exchange a knowing look.

I stuff the manna into my mouth and enjoy it as the others swallow their goo.

Then I turn to Bebe. "So. Where is my sister?"

CHAPTER SEVENTEEN

BEBE PUTS down her tube and sighs. "Asha lives with the Escapists."

"I thought so," Valerian says grimly.

"It makes sense," my father says with a frown. "But I don't like it."

"Who or what are the Escapists?" I ask, puzzled.

Bebe looks at me, then at Valerian and Maxwell.

"Bailey doesn't remember much about her life here," Valerian explains.

"A black window?" Bebe asks.

"I couldn't locate one," I say.

Bebe strokes her wrinkled chin. "Asha also has a memory gap. She doesn't remember Bailey—and more importantly, Max and Lia—and we couldn't locate a black window in her case either." She studies my father with an unreadable expression. "My theory about Asha's memory loss is that it was caused by the pain of having seen both her parents become Overtaken." Her gaze shifts to me. "That's probably the case for the both of you."

She might be right. That could indeed be the reason for my memory loss. My parents suddenly became slaves to an evil deity who wanted me dead. I'm an adult, and I wish I could forget all about it.

I pick up my tube and squirt some of the goo into my mouth. "Let's get back to the Escapists."

Bebe looks at Valerian. "Any suggestions on how to best explain them?"

"Start earlier." He swallows some of the goo. "Maybe tell her the ancient history of Soma."

Bebe looks thoughtful. "I can do that. Just bear in mind, this history is more like a legend. We don't know how much is fact or fiction."

I nod.

She waves her hand to encompass our surroundings. "As should be abundantly clear, we're a space colony."

"So it *is* a spaceship," I say.

"Of sorts," she says. "It was designed to sustain a population indefinitely, so in that way, not very different from a planet. Just smaller."

I look around in wonder. "Is Soma flying somewhere specific? Is the plan to arrive at a distant star?"

"Sadly, no," Valerian says.

"We're orbiting a planet," Bebe adds.

"A dead planet," Maxwell says darkly. "Our

ancestors' home and the first world that Collywobbles destroyed."

My head spins.

Bebe eats more of her food, the form of which makes more sense in the context of a spaceship. "Some legends also say our world is where he's from," she says. "They claim he was a dreamwalker who made humans worship him—and that the purpose of Soma was not just to escape, but to produce a dreamwalker powerful enough to defeat him one day."

I realize my mouth is open, so I shut it before some space bug flies in.

Maxwell finishes his tube of goo. "They say the way Collywobbles became what he is today was by building a device that locked his brain in a state of perpetual REM sleep. His body was discarded in the process—and therefore, should he die in the dream world, he'd be gone."

Well, that's good to know. "What's the best way to kill him?" I ask eagerly.

"Beheading would do it," Bebe says.

"Except that anyone who's gotten close enough to try that trick has been Overtaken," Maxwell says bitterly.

Right. He's speaking from personal experience. "Then what's the solution? How do you behead him if it's not safe to get close to him?"

"Something to do with that business of Two as One," Maxwell says. "Hopefully."

"Right," I say. "And that brings us back to the original question of Asha."

"I'm almost there," Bebe says. "Early Soma colonists wanted to return home, and that meant defeating Collywobbles. There was a lot of training to that end, and some even married in ways that led to boosting dreamwalker powers in their children. After a while, a group of Soma residents got sick of such an onerous life. They didn't want to deal with the big goal. They felt cooped up by the size of the colony, sick of the bland food and everything else. They decided it was unfair to be born into such a life, and that the rest of the Cogniverse should deal with Collywobbles on their own. As a result, they created a solipsistic dream world for themselves, and they live out their lives in there instead of the real world. Whenever they wake up, a group of illusionists use their powers to make the whole thing seamless for them, and they themselves use memory erasure to forget that the rest of Soma and Collywobbles exist. If they had a motto, it would be 'ignorance is bliss.'"

I scratch my head. "And they're the Escapists? Why would Asha want to live with them?"

"She didn't. We put her there," Bebe says. "The story we wanted everyone to believe was that the two of you were killed. We couldn't maintain that falsehood if she were prancing around Soma."

That makes sense. When I was in Valerian's black window, he told me he hadn't seen her growing up and that she probably was in a part of Soma separated from the rest.

He was right.

I leap to my feet. "Can we go get her now?"

Bebe squeezes the last of her tube into her mouth and stands up as well. "Let's."

She hands the gun to Valerian and leads us out of the cafeteria building. As we walk, she tells us how the ranks of the Escapists have grown recently and warns me about what to do when we reach them, which basically boils down to avoiding mentioning anything unpleasant that could turn a dream into a nightmare.

"Why does the rest of Soma put up with them?" I ask as we get to the forest area.

"They go out of their way to avoid nightmares, so they never get Overtaken," Bebe says. "Basically, they're harmless, so nobody minds their existence."

We walk onto a clearing, and I swallow my next question, too fascinated by what I see.

A large squadron of guards with guns stands around a circular moat dug up in the soil. All their guns are pointed at the very center—where a single gate stands, one that looks just like the ones at the hubs, only lonesome.

I step on a dry branch, and they turn, pointing the guns at me.

"At ease," Bebe says.

"Yes, ma'am," they reply in unison, then turn back and point their guns back at the gate.

"Keep up the good work," Bebe tells them and waves for us to follow her.

As we proceed deeper into the forest, I recall her saying that the Overtaken have come from the Otherlands. Sounds like they arrive to a warm reception. Bebe explains that the guards don't even bother shooting if only one or two Overtaken come through the gate. Since every guard is an illusionist, they work together to make the Overtaken—and their master—see something that isn't there. Something that makes them kill each other.

Eventually, we come out to an area that appears to be a clone of the place we came from—which is now in the sky from this vantage point.

A guard is patrolling nearby.

Bebe points her hand at him, and he falls down, instantly in REM sleep.

Valerian raises an eyebrow.

"Just so they don't ask too many questions," Bebe explains and heads toward a small spherical structure.

When we get there, she plays with some machine, and when I ask what she's doing, she says, "Disabling the cameras. Again, don't feel like answering questions."

How crappy is the security here that she can just turn off cameras willy-nilly? Unless she's a hacker, like Felix?

Bebe leads us farther in until we stop next to a chrome door with controls similar to those for the cameras. I can feel three people in REM sleep inside the room.

Bebe points her hand at the door. There's a thud, and I can feel a fourth person enter REM sleep.

She fiddles with the controls, and the door slides away. We step over a sleeping illusionist that Bebe has knocked out with her powers and walk inside—only to stare at my sister and her family in horror.

Asha, Kojo, and their daughter, Chloe, are hooked up to a web of machines that look like close relatives of the ones that keep Mom alive.

Except this family isn't in a coma. They're just sleeping.

I fight the urge to rip the tubes and cables away from them. "Is this the medical bay?"

Bebe shakes her head. "The equipment is here to feed them and make sure they're hydrated."

The gear hooked up to Asha begins vibrating and jostling her around.

I look at our grandmother.

"That equipment was originally used to stave off muscle degeneration when the colony's artificial gravity wasn't on," she explains. "Without it, they wouldn't be able to function upon return to the real world."

"I hope they have this in the medical bay," I say. "Mom could use it."

"Don't worry, they'll build up her muscles there," Bebe says confidently. "The one positive side effect of dealing with the Escapists is our competence in this area."

I examine my sister with concern. "Do they never, ever wake up?"

Bebe gives me a confused look. "They couldn't have exactly made a baby in the dream world, could they?"

Great. I almost walked into the-birds-and-the-bees talk with my grandmother.

I scan the gear attached to my twin. "Why use the machines then?"

"Prophylactic," she replies. "They take a cocktail of substances to stay in the dream world for as long as they can, so muscle atrophy and nutrient deficiency can become a concern."

"I see. And she agreed to this life?"

"It's better than exile from Soma," Maxwell says softly.

I could argue but opt not to.

"They're there willingly." There's a note of defensiveness in Bebe's voice.

I scratch the back of my head. "What I don't get is how they keep the whole 'ignorance is bliss' attitude while they're awake."

"That was a challenge, but they solved it. In exchange for being able to visit the dream world, Escapist illusionists do their best to make the awake time—what they call Contemplative Domain—go smoother for the dreamwalkers. For example, they make sure no Escapist sees Soma as it really is, with the unusual sky and all."

Right. She's already mentioned something like that. "How do they maintain a dream world that's shared by so many people?" I ask.

"Actually, the dream changes, but there's still coordination involved. It's one of the things they also deal with while awake."

"I'm glad we came while they're asleep," I say. "I'm curious about their world."

Valerian squeezes my shoulder. "Careful, now. I don't want you to like it so much you'd abandon reality."

I laugh. "Even if it's the most utopian heaven imaginable, the machines would be a deal breaker for me. Besides"—I make eye contact with him—"there are things in the real world I wouldn't want to leave behind."

"That's sweet," Bebe says. "Now, is everyone ready to go in?"

We all nod.

She gestures at nearby cots. "Valerian, you should lie down."

Valerian obeys, and she puts him into REM sleep. Then she lies down on the nearby cot and extends her hand toward him. "See you in my dreams."

"I'm going in," my father says, gesturing toward Bebe.

I also make a remote dream connection with my grandmother and dive in.

WHEN I SHOW up in my dream palace, Pom is there, waving his furry paw at me.

"You're in for a treat," I say. "We're about to meet my twin."

He flies up to my shoulder, his fur turning a deep golden color. "Let's hurry up."

I get us to the tower of sleepers and turn my head to look into Pom's guileless eyes. "Would you mind staying invisible?"

"Why?"

"I don't know what the Escapists might find unpleasant."

The tips of his ears redden. "You think they might find *me* unpleasant?"

"I doubt it," I say, making him invisible myself. "But they do seem crazy, so who knows."

"I'll be quiet," he says solemnly.

"Thanks."

I locate my grandmother in the tower of sleepers, touch her forehead, and prepare to see the dream world that the Escapists prefer to reality.

CHAPTER EIGHTEEN

WE'RE on the bottom of the ocean.

Bebe, Valerian, and my father are breathing effortlessly, so I let myself inhale the water. Instead of causing pain to my lungs, as it would in the real world, this liquid pleasantly fills me up and leaves a scent of salty ocean surf in my nostrils.

"I guess it's nice to completely forget reality sometimes," I say, and my voice sounds normal despite the liquid around us.

Valerian looks up. "You can say that again."

I follow his gaze, and my breath catches as I take in the view above us.

If this were a real ocean bottom, everything would be pitch black. These depths, however, are lit up like a shallow coral reef on a sunny day.

But the light—and the lack of crushing water pressure—are just the beginnings of the wonders. There's an underwater city here, and it sprawls from horizon to horizon. With its floating castle-like skyscrapers and mind-numbingly large scale, it puts even Gomorrah to shame.

"Welcome to the Water Domain," Bebe says. "It's Asha's favorite."

"There are other domains?" I strain to see above the water.

"So many I've lost count." Bebe raises her arms above her head like a diver and launches up, torpedo-style.

Valerian, my father, and I follow.

Bebe stops her ascent next to one of the largest castle-like buildings and floats there until we catch up.

"This is Asha's home," she says, gesturing for us to get inside.

We end up in a room the size of a large theme park —much larger than the castle was from the outside.

"They're probably in the living room," Bebe says and zooms through the water toward a pair of doors the size of five-story buildings.

She pushes them open, and I'm startled to see that the next room lacks water.

"The Escapists don't bother with realism," Bebe says when she notices me staring at the spot where a wall of water simply stands in defiance of common sense.

Without comment, I step from the watery room into the air of the next one.

Consistent with the lack of realism Bebe mentioned, I'm not wet in the slightest. Nor are the others when they join me.

Apart from being waterless, this room is just as big as the prior one, making it even less likely that it could be inside the castle we entered. Oh, and the views from the floor-to-ceiling windows are those of a desert, not of any kind of watery domain.

There's also another city in the distance, one that looks like a mirage come to life.

"That's the Sand Domain," Bebe explains. "Kojo's favorite."

She takes a leisurely step forward but somehow ends up miles away from us.

I step forward as I would in the real world and end up next to Bebe.

Forget realism. It's actually possible the Escapists go out of their way to defy it.

The next room's windows must look out onto the Snow or Winter Domain, on account of all the frozen wilderness and the city made of ice in the distance. After that, we're back in the Water Domain, swimming in a "room" the size of Manhattan.

"This is the living room," Bebe says two rooms later. The view out of the window here is that of breathtaking volcanoes.

Is this the Seismic Domain? Through several enormous windows, I can see a floating city in the clouds, right in the path of volcanic eruptions that don't seem to harm it one bit.

But not all windows are see-through here.

Some of them are black.

Interesting.

"Bebe," says a child's voice. "You're back!"

My niece appears in front of us not unlike Pom sometimes does. Her adorable curls defy gravity, making the top of her head look like a perfect sphere. On the very top of the hairdo is a tiara with diamonds so big a royal family would kill to possess it, and a few inches above the tiara hovers what looks like a halo, but in the shape of an infinity symbol.

"Hi, honey," Bebe says, smiling at her. "Where's Mommy and Daddy?"

Chloe closes her eyes for a second, then grins as she opens them. "Now they know you're here."

Does she not see the rest of us?

I wave a hand.

No reaction.

"Thank you," Bebe says. "How are things going?"

Still ignoring us, Chloe takes off her tiara and bites into it, gleefully crunching on a large diamond and some of the metal. "I'm studying elliptic geometry."

"And?" Bebe asks.

The missing piece of the tiara grows back, and Chloe puts it back on her head. "On a sphere, the sum of the angles of a triangle is not equal to one hundred and eighty degrees." As she speaks, a large sphere appears in front of us, with a triangle outlined.

"That's right," Bebe says, nodding approvingly. "And, if memory serves, there are no parallel lines."

I scratch my head, and that seems to finally draw my niece's attention.

"Such strange constructs," she says, looking at me

and Maxwell. "She looks identical to Mommy, and that man also shares a few of her features. But that last one"—her gaze shifts to Valerian—"doesn't look like her at all. Is it an art project?"

"They're not constructs." Bebe playfully pinches Chloe's cheek. "They're real people."

My niece's amber eyes widen. "Newbies?"

"Even better," Bebe says. "They're guests."

Now we have Chloe's complete and undivided attention, especially me. "Why did you decide to look like Mommy?" she asks, examining me like a bug under a microscope. "Do you admire her that much?"

I give Bebe a questioning look. Is saying "I'm your aunt" considered unpleasant information that we're supposed to avoid in this world? Or is the unpleasant info bit only meant for any non-family Escapists?

Two new people poof into existence between us and the girl.

My pulse leaps.

It's my twin and her husband, Kojo, both also with infinity halos above their heads—must be an Escapist thing.

Smiling at Bebe, Asha looks everyone over curiously, her gaze lingering on me.

"Nice choice of face." Her voice sounds just like mine, only a little uncanny in the way voice recordings are. "What do you really look like?"

Bebe's eyes are misty as she steps forward and clasps my twin's hands. "Asha… I want you to meet your father and twin sister."

CHAPTER NINETEEN

CHLOE'S MOUTH SLACKENS, Kojo's eyes widen, and Asha is blinking so fast her lashes look in danger of falling off.

"Father?" my twin repeats, her gaze darting between me and Maxwell as she twists out of our grandmother's hold. "Sister?"

Bebe solemnly nods.

My throat feels swollen and tight, so I just stand there, taking in Asha's reactions.

A diamond throne appears behind her, and she sags into it.

Kojo steps forward, recovering from shock. "Valerian. Long time no see."

That's right. They were besties.

Valerian claps him on the shoulder, and they embrace while Asha darts a glance at one of the black windows. "Why don't I remember them? Did I lock them away?" You can almost hear the unasked, "And why?"

My throat tightens further. On some level, I was hoping that seeing each other would unlock the memories we seem to be missing, but I guess no such luck.

"I told you about them," Bebe says. "You must've locked those conversations away."

The throne disappears as Asha pushes up to her feet. "I don't understand. How can this be real?"

"I remember Bailey, hon," Kojo says, turning toward her. "And your father. I also told you about them…"

She swallows. "Must've locked that away, too."

Bebe nods at the black windows. "How about you and Kojo unlock all your memories and wake up so we can talk?"

"I guess," Asha says, looking shaken. "Is he a relative too?" She points at Valerian.

Kojo frowns. "You don't recognize him, either? That's Valerian, our friend from childhood. I mention him all the time."

Her jaw firms. "You're right. I've locked too much away."

Bebe and Kojo exchange a knowing look, then Kojo says, "We'll be out in a few."

Clasping his wife's hand, he leads her to one of the black windows, and as they disappear into it, Bebe jolts everyone awake.

———

BACK IN THE REAL WORLD, I wipe sweat from my brow.

Maxwell stands up, looking equally devastated. "That didn't go as I expected."

"What did you expect?" I ask.

Bebe also gets to her feet. "Give them some time. In fact, why don't we wait outside the building?"

I let them herd me out, my mind still spinning from everything that happened.

Once outside, I pace until the door creaks open, and Asha and her family step out. Here, in the real world, she looks a little bit older, her body a little rounder than mine. Stepping up to me, she touches my face, like a blind person.

Not sure what to do with my hands, I touch her face too, my heart thudding with bittersweet pain.

"All I remember is what Kojo and Bebe told me about you," she whispers, staring into my eyes. "They said our mother stole you away. I don't doubt we're sisters, but I still don't remember you and I don't know why."

My mouth feels as dry as the Sand Domain. "I don't remember anything either. All I know about our childhood is what I've seen in other people's memories."

She drops her hands and steps back. "Did we lock it away?"

"Not through a black window," I say quietly. "At least none that I've found."

She faces our father. "They said you were Overtaken."

Maxwell winces. "I beat it. I'm sorry I didn't come back. I made myself forget everything. I now see how much of a mistake that was."

Asha's face looks just like mine does in the mirror when I'm on the verge of a mental breakdown. "What about our mother?" she demands. "Did she beat it? Is she here too?"

"She's on my side of Soma," Bebe says.

For the first time, I realize no one is making Asha and her family think Soma doesn't exist, and they're okay with it.

"You know about the real world?" I ask my sister.

Bebe stands up straighter. "Asha and her family aren't your typical Escapists."

"We let ourselves recall Soma and the rest of it when we're awake," Asha says. Looking at her daughter, she sternly adds, "And we tell no one about it, understood?"

"Yes, Mommy." Chloe winds a curl around her little finger. "I've never told anyone anything and never will."

"That's a good girl." Asha looks back at me. "Why didn't our mother come with you?"

"She couldn't." I dampen my lips. "She's in a coma."

Asha's eyes widen.

"How about we explain more on the way to the medical bay?" Bebe says.

No one objects, and we head in the direction of the nearby forest.

"Valerian, can you make Asha and her family invisible to the guards?" Bebe asks. "Still don't want those questions."

Valerian—who's been talking in hushed tones with Kojo—nods and presumably does as Bebe asks.

Maxwell chats up Chloe while Asha and I fall back a little.

"Tell me about your life," we say in unison.

After a chuckle, we say, still in unison, "You first."

I stay silent this time, but she does as well.

We both laugh.

"You're a guest here," Asha says, finally breaking the strange synchronicity. "I'll go first."

I listen greedily as she tells me about her life as far back as she can recall.

She and our grandmother lived in an apartment on the Escapists' side of Soma. In the beginning, my sister would visit their dream world without the use of drugs and machines—mainly to kill the time as she waited for our grandmother to come back from her business on the other side of Soma.

At some point, Kojo started visiting. Our grandmother arranged it so that he was one of the few people on Soma who didn't believe Asha dead. With time, she and Kojo found the Escapists' world a fun getaway and spent more and more time there, eventually using all the methods to extend the stay, just like the rest of Escapists.

When they were old enough, they got married, and sometime later, their love gave them Chloe—who Asha thinks is the brightest and cutest being in the universe.

"That sounds like a charmed life," I say. "Like a perpetual honeymoon."

Asha agrees but reiterates the difference between her family and "normal" Escapists. She and Kojo don't permanently forget everything about their pre-Escapist lives; they do it selectively, and only when asleep. Also, they visit the other side of Soma on occasion, with the help of a Bebe-approved illusionist who makes them invisible.

"I'm really sorry I knew nothing about you when we met in the dream world," she says. "I locked away the memories of our grandmother telling me about you and our parents because it's just too painful to know you have family you can't remember."

"I don't blame you," I say. "If I knew how to create black windows, I'd probably lock away a thing or two."

She stops and gives me an incredulous look. "You don't know how to lock away memories?"

"I probably don't know a lot of basic dreamwalking techniques," I say and launch into my own story—one that starts with our mother not teaching me anything about dreamwalking or speaking about the past.

Since Asha does seem able to handle "unpleasantness," I don't sugarcoat anything. I explain how Mom thought she'd killed Asha, so she locked away those memories. I go over my theory as well: that on some level, though Mom couldn't recall why, she'd feared I'd dreamwalk in her and stumble onto this horrible secret.

Asha grimaces. "Our poor mom. If I thought I'd killed Chloe, I'd end myself right then and there."

"She couldn't," I say. "She had me. Well, she couldn't until I was old enough." Chest tightening, I explain about Mom's suicide attempt and my inadvertent role in it.

We pass by the moat-ringed gate and the squadron of guards protecting it in a heavy silence. Meanwhile, the conversation between Valerian and Kojo grows more boisterous, and I overhear Chloe grilling Maxwell with endless random questions.

"Tell me more," Asha urges, so I do. I tell her about the good memories with our mother on Gomorrah and about my efforts to keep her alive and undo the damage done by the car accident.

"What about him?" Asha asks in the middle of my story about Necronia. She nods in Maxwell's direction. "You didn't mention our father at all."

"Right. That's a whole other thing. We met only a few days ago, but it wasn't until earlier today that I realized who he is." That leads into yet another complicated story, which I do my best to cover as we step out of the forest and walk toward the structure we visited earlier.

"Bebe did mention something about a prophecy," she says when I finish telling her about why we came to Soma. "It just never made sense to me. You and I are supposed to defeat Phobetor?"

"Call him Collywobbles, but yes."

"How?"

"I don't know. That's just the prophecy. I'm not sure how I feel about it. I don't think of myself as a hero. Do you?"

She chuckles and shakes her head. "Hardly. So you have no idea what Two as One means?"

"In our father's memories, he and Mom talked about something we did as kids that sounded like it. The hope was that you'd remember what it was."

She frowns. "I have no clue."

"Me neither," I say.

Bebe holds the door for us, and we begin to navigate the corridors to the medical bay.

Asha lets everyone go ahead again and falls into step next to me. "You know," she says quietly, "my whole life I've felt like a piece of me was missing."

A bittersweet ache pierces my chest. "Me too."

"Could the act of our reuniting be Two as One?" she asks hopefully. "Is there any way we can consult the seer about it?"

"He foretold that Valerian and I would never see him again. So unless he talks to us via proxy, I don't see that happening."

We enter a room covered to the brim with medical equipment. Must be the medical bay. And indeed, I spot Mom here. She's out of her portable bed and hooked up the way Asha and her family were.

Asha walks over to peer at Mom's face, her

expression so full of longing it gives me a knot in my throat.

Chloe tugs on Bebe's shirt. "That's your daughter who's my grandmother?"

Eyes puffy, Bebe nods.

"And she's asleep but not dreaming?" my niece presses.

"Something like that," Bebe says thickly. She looks at Asha. "Can *you* push her into REM sleep?"

My sister lays a hand on Mom's arm and closes her eyes, visibly concentrating.

"She's one of the best dreamwalkers on Soma," Bebe whispers into my ear. "Living with the Escapists has allowed her to hone her skills to perfection."

Asha opens her eyes. She loks beyond disappointed. "It didn't work. Should I risk going in like this?"

"No," Bebe, Maxwell, and Kojo say at the same time.

She rounds on them, eyes narrowing. "Then what do we do?"

"You and Bailey need to prepare," Bebe says. "Work together to figure out what Two as One could be."

Asha scoffs. "Prepare to defeat Collywobbles? You don't ask for much, do you?"

I put a hand on her shoulder. "How about we start by filling in gaps in my dreamwalking techniques?"

A faint smile touches my sister's lips. "All right."

"I'll help," Maxwell says.

"And me," Bebe says.

"I'll take all the help I can get," I say. "When do you want to start?"

"Now." Asha lies down on a nearby cot. "I go first."

Nodding approvingly, Bebe puts her into REM sleep, while I get comfortable on a nearby cot.

"See you later," I tell everyone and eagerly jump into my sister's dreams.

CHAPTER TWENTY

AS SOON AS I show up in my dream palace, I make my hair fiery, grab Pom, and teleport to the tower of sleepers.

"She looks just like you," Pom says, flitting around as I lean over my sister.

"Want to come meet her?" I ask.

He turns purple and nods so vigorously I worry he might hurt his neck.

Smiling, I take his paw in my left hand and touch Asha's wrist.

———

I STARE AROUND IN CONFUSION.

Instead of Asha's dreams, I'm back in my dream palace lobby.

Or not.

The colors differ, my collection of impossible shapes isn't here, but the basic layout is the same.

Also, Asha is here, gaping at Pom, who's hovering over me.

"Where are we?" I ask her.

"I call this my dream castle," she says proudly. "Now what the heck is that?" She points at Pom.

I hastily explain about Pom and then say, "Your castle looks just like my palace."

"Your what?"

"The place I appear when I first go into the dream world of another person," I say. "It's also where I go when I realize I'm dreaming myself."

She blinks. "It's the same for me. I realized I was dreaming, remembered why, and waited for you here."

I take a closer look at my surroundings.

Colors and shapes aside, every tile and every piece of marble is the same as in my dream palace. Up in the ceiling is the exact same mosaic depicting an archery-target-like mandala made out of multicolored glass.

The main difference is that she calls hers a castle.

"We must've designed this together as children." I stroke Pom's fur as he lands on my shoulder. "Before the memory loss."

She hesitantly approaches and touches Pom's ear. "It has to be that."

"Does yours also have a tower of sleepers?" Pom asks, his huge lavender eyes glued to my sister. "And a memory gallery?"

I explain what those are, and Asha grins widely,

then takes us to a clone of my tower of sleepers, only larger.

"That's a lot of connections," I say, examining the never-ending floors. "And they're all asleep right now."

"Those are my fellow Escapists," she says.

Ah, right. She woke up ahead of schedule.

I take her to my tower of sleepers, and she can't believe how alike they are, size aside.

I show her my memory gallery next, and she takes us to her version.

The paintings are obviously different, as are the memories they replay, but the layout of the room itself is the same. Ditto for the style of the frames and the floors.

"Can I experience some of your memories?" Asha asks shyly.

My pulse speeds up. "Can I see yours?"

She nods excitedly, and we spend a while sharing our best memories. I get to experience some truly amazing things—like giving birth and nursing a baby—as well as countless precious moments with Bebe.

"Thank you," Asha says after she's done with the last memory in my gallery, the one where I broke a vase that later turned out to have prints of both Asha's and my hands. "I feel like I just got to know our mother."

I pet Pom's furry feet. "And seeing your memories made me feel like all those things had happened to me."

Grinning, she makes her hair fiery to match mine. "Seems like being twins, our experiences are that much more compatible. Kojo and I experimented with this a bit, and when I saw some events from his point of view, it was jarring."

"I'm not surprised," Pom chimes in, his fur turning golden. "You have the same mannerisms, and the way you talk is the same. Even little things like your smiles are—"

"We're monozygotic twins," I say. "We have the same exact genes, and we lived together for the first few years of our lives. I'm surprised we're not finishing—"

"Each other's sentences," Asha says with a wide grin.

Pom rolls his eyes with a melodramatic sigh. "Even what passes for your sense of humor is similar."

I grab him by the feet and tickle his chin until he apologizes.

"He reminds me of Chloe," Asha says with a grin.

"Oh yeah?" Ears turning a light shade of orange, Pom escapes from my clutches and lands at her feet. "Can I meet her?"

"She'd love that," Asha says, grinning down at him. "But business first."

"Right," I say. "You're supposed to be teaching me something I don't know."

She nods. "How about you tell me what you can already do?"

I start by explaining how I use my powers for therapy, and how I take jobs pulling out memories from people. I then tell her about my fight with the Nutcracker and what I've learned more recently— including how to unlock black windows, duplicate myself, enter dreams from a distance, and push people into REM sleep.

"That's pretty solid." Asha makes the room around us match her enormous living room in the Escapist world. "I think we'd better start with the more difficult tricks and work our way down."

"Like what?" I ask.

"Voila." She shrinks until she's the size of Pom. "Have you ever played with perspective like this?"

Pom and I just gape at her diminutive form.

"I'm ashamed to admit this idea has never occurred to me," I say. "Not even after reading *Alice in Wonderland*."

Asha gives me a confused look and in a high-pitched voice asks, "Who's Alice?"

"Oh, just a book on this primitive world I frequently go to," I say. "Don't worry about it."

"Ah, okay," she says. "I wouldn't beat yourself up for not trying this particular idea. It's not very practical, especially given how you've been using your power. Besides, if you did try, you'd find it harder than it seems. Chloe hasn't been able to master it, and even Kojo is terrible at it."

Really? She's right in that it doesn't seem that hard, in theory.

Asha grows back to her normal size—and keeps growing until she's a giant.

I look up enviously and will myself to grow as well.

Nothing happens.

Asha shrinks to her normal size. "To do this, you have to picture yourself made out of molecules."

Closing my eyes, I do as she says, visualizing myself as made from molecules of water, oxygen, DNA, hemoglobin, ATP, digestive enzymes, cholesterol, and as many other things as I can recall from my chemistry and biology classes. My fear of germs works to my advantage here. There have been times when I've pictured getting attacked by bacteria and viruses in a mental exercise that's quite similar to this.

"Now grow the molecules as you would a random object," she instructs.

Hmm, okay. The number of cells in the body is something like thirty trillion, and each cell can contain up to two trillion molecules. That makes the total number of my molecules something unfathomable, like a septillion.

I will those septillions to grow.

When I open my eyes, I'm the same size.

I repeat the exercise, but it doesn't work on the second try either. Or third.

"Use your emotions to your advantage," Asha says.

Pom turns light orange. "Emotions help with dreamwalking?"

"Of course." Asha shrinks to his size, then goes back to normal. "There's a strong connection between dreams and emotions in general."

Of course. I can't believe I haven't figured this out on my own. It makes so much sense. "You're right. I did some of my best dreamwalking when I was fighting the

Nutcracker, and I was teeming with emotions that time. Well, one specific one: fear."

Asha smiles mischievously, and we appear in a new room, one that looks like the largest dojo in the history of martial arts. "Let's leverage your fear."

Before I can say anything, a throwing star pierces my shoulder.

"Hey, that hurts!"

With a speed almost too fast to perceive, Asha manifests another throwing star in her hand and launches it at me again.

I dodge, then materialize a hundred-pound jar of coconut pudding above my sister's head and let it fall.

She neutralizes my delicious attack and makes a sword telekinetically jump into her hand from the nearby displays.

Pom watches us, his fur pitch black. But hey, at least he hasn't disappeared on me this time.

Asha leaps at me, sword raised.

With a move we practiced for the subdream battles, Pom jumps onto my wrist and becomes a furry katana —just in time for me to parry Asha's thrust.

She delivers a flurry of attacks.

My breathing speeds up.

"Are you scared yet?" she asks.

"A little."

She stops and grows to the size of a giant, sword and all.

"Grow if you want to live," she booms and slashes down with her sword.

CHAPTER TWENTY-ONE

RATIONALLY, I know Asha must be bluffing. Yet I'm afraid. Very afraid. I think it's a combination of the adrenaline coursing through my system from the fight and the lizard part of my brain reacting to a being that large swinging a sword at me.

A horrific thought flits through my mind. What if she doesn't know I'll go insane if she kills me? Could that knowledge be something she'd locked away and didn't recover today?

Okay, if fear was the desired goal, I've got plenty of it now. Maybe too much.

Channeling it as well as I can, I will my molecules to grow.

There's a moment of vertigo, then I find myself blocking Asha's sword with my Pom katana.

We're the same size.

I look at the room around us. Yep. Everything else is tiny.

Suddenly and without my willful participation, I shrink back to my usual size.

Asha does as well, then changes the dojo to the previous living room and evaporates her sword. "I'm so proud of you. Few people manage to do this on their first day."

Pom separates from my wrist and lands on my shoulder. "You grew me too," he says excitedly. "That was awesome."

I wipe sweat from my forehead and jump out of my body to heal my shoulder. "You're a part of me, so that was a freebie," I tell Pom when I return. I look sheepishly at Asha. "Despite all that fear, I couldn't stay big for even two seconds."

My sister manifests a throne for each of us and plops into hers. "Part of the reason staying big is so tricky is that it's not rooted in everyday experience. On top of that, when you're big or small, you have to keep worrying about proportions at all times—which is a lot of complicated math. Don't worry, though. Over the coming days and weeks, we'll have you practice holding size variations."

I sit down on my throne. "Will you need to nearly kill me each time?"

She shrugs. "What other emotions do you want to leverage?"

"I don't know. But you do know actually killing me would be bad, right?"

"Of course," she says. "You weren't in any danger. I'm just that good of a dreamwalker."

"Modest too." I grin at her. "Can the great dreamwalker master teach the lowly student something else?"

She rubs the diamonds in the armrests of her throne. "Have you ever tried pushing people into REM sleep from inside the dream world? Or across large distances?"

Pom flies onto my lap, lavender eyes wide. "You can do that?"

"Yep," Asha says. "I can put anyone on Soma to sleep from here."

"How?" I ask.

She shrugs. "Just focus on the person in question and do what you would do from nearby."

"Wow," I say. "Can I try?"

She grins. "Do it to Bebe. That shouldn't be too challenging. She's in the same room with us, just in the waking world."

Rubbing my hands together, I close my eyes and picture my grandmother in enough detail to create a dream construct. But instead of making a fake Bebe, I will the real one to go into REM sleep.

Did that work?

"You girls miss me already?" Bebe's voice says.

I open my eyes.

Score. My grandmother is here. I can't believe this worked on the very first try. And it's even better than I expected—instead of appearing in my dream palace, Bebe is right here.

She shifts her appearance to that of her younger

self. "I assume you bothered me because you figured out how to be Two as One?"

Asha and I exchange guilty glances.

"They didn't really talk about that," Pom says.

"Traitor," I mutter.

Asha jumps off her throne. "How about we work on that now?"

"I'm game. What do we do?"

"I have no idea." Asha quirks an eyebrow. "Bebe, do you have suggestions?"

"I think you should start with the most direct understanding of Two as One," Bebe says.

"And that is?" Asha asks.

"Become a single being," Bebe replies.

We gape at her.

"Can that even be done?" Asha asks.

Bebe shrugs. "Your parents tried it."

"And?" I ask.

She closes her eyes, and a second later, Maxwell joins us.

"Tell them how you and Lia tried to become a single being in the dream world," Bebe orders.

Maxwell frowns. "It never worked. We'd just get punishingly tired after each attempt."

"What fun," Asha says. "Can't wait to experience that."

"Where we failed, you two may succeed," Maxwell says. "After all, at one point in time, you were the same being—a single fertilized egg."

"That was before we could dream," Asha says.

"Exactly," I chime in. "Let's not forget how that egg split into two separate embryos, and how those embryos eventually ended up living pretty different lives. Even if this is something we did as kids, there's no reason to think it will still work."

"Well, I'm curious to see how it goes," Bebe says.

Asha approaches me. "What do you think?"

"For Mom, I'll try anything. Even if it seems kind of weird."

"And creepy," she says. "But let's try it."

"How?" I ask.

"Let's do that same molecule trick from earlier, but tell yours to mix with mine."

"You should hug as you do it," Pom suggests.

Shrugging, I hug her—which feels nice and soothing.

I close my eyes and do my best to imagine us becoming a single person. I visualize the molecules intermixing as Asha suggested, a task made easier by the fact that our DNA is the same.

Nothing happens. That is, until I feel really woozy.

Asha's arms are no longer around me, and someone audibly gasps.

I open my eyes—or maybe our eyes.

Nope.

Asha is still separate from me. She's just stepped away and is dry-heaving.

I also feel sick but hold myself together better.

"Did it work?" I ask Maxwell and Bebe when the

worst of the nausea passes. "Did we merge even for a moment?"

"No," he says.

"Not even a little bit," she says.

"Don't do that again." Pom's fur is a dingy yellow. "It made me sick."

Asha inhales a deep breath and lets it out slowly. "There's no way we did that successfully as children."

A wave of exhaustion hits me. To make sure I don't fall on my butt, I make a lounge chair and plop into it. Before Asha's knees buckle, I make a chair appear under her as well.

"Thanks." She sinks into it and looks at Maxwell. "When you said it would be punishingly tiring, you weren't kidding."

"Sounds like that will be the end of training for today," Bebe says. "Bailey should rest."

"I agree." Maxwell looks at me worriedly. "You've had a crazy day."

I chuckle humorlessly. "Oh, I've been merely saved from a deadly virus just in time to fight hordes of the Overtaken. I call that Tuesday."

"I've arranged a room for you," Bebe says. "You should go and rest."

"I will," I say. "But could you two teach me something else first? Something quick and easy?"

Bebe gives Maxwell an expectant look.

"How about we start with some theory?" he asks.

I shrug.

"As you probably know, keeping track of details is one of the hardest parts of dreamwalking," he says. "You're building worlds in your mind, so your ability to remember details is one of the limiting factors."

"She's just played with growing big and small," Asha chimes in. "So we've touched on what you're talking about."

"Good," Maxwell says. "So here's a practical tip: You can find ways to make it easier on your mind while you expand your power."

I eye him in confusion. "Are you talking about mnemonics?"

"Something even more natural," Maxwell says. "Being social beings, we're already very good when it comes to our memories of other people."

"Right. And?"

He waves a hand, and we find ourselves in a valley where a crowd of people stands. "One way for you to use a lot of your power yet not overtax your mind is to utilize dream characters of people you know to help you."

I scan the crowd and whistle. "If I'd used something like this on the Nutcracker, I would've beaten him that much quicker."

"There you go," Maxwell says. "Keep in mind the constructs can be friends, enemies, or even fictional characters—so long as you can imagine them being real and therefore give them a dream life that would feel almost independent from you."

Asha nods approvingly. "This isn't something I've experimented with, but I will now."

I consider what Maxwell is saying. I've used dream characters as dream lovers and in other ways to entertain myself, but I've never thought about weaponizing them.

But why not?

With barely any effort at all, I manifest as many people as I can, starting with those closest to me—like Valerian, Felix, Ariel, Itzel, and Kit.

As soon as they appear, they begin to talk among themselves as dream characters often do.

Maxwell is right. I don't feel any drain on my attention.

Okay, let's push this. Since they don't even have to be among the living, I manifest Fabian, Edith, and Stanislav.

They appear and join the conversation with Felix and Ariel.

Seeing them makes me a little sad, but I busy myself with adding some of my patients and favorite celebrities to my growing army.

It works just as well as with friends. Each new person greets the others, and they gleefully join forces.

This could be fun.

I begin to manifest fictional characters from different media on both Gomorrah and Earth. Soon, the likes of Joygasm Troglodyte, Dracula, Robin Hood, Frankenstein, Zorro, and Tarzan join the fray, followed by whichever other heroes and villains come to mind.

Next, I throw in gods of different mythologies into the mix, like Thor, Athena, and Morrigan.

Last but not least, I add my favorite video game characters.

"Good," my father says. "Let's see if you feel any strain on your resources as the battle ensues."

Before I can ask what battle, his crowd of characters roars a war cry and rushes at mine.

I watch the clash yet feel no more tired than I already am—which is, granted, pretty tired.

In mere seconds, his army slaughters mine.

I look at the dead and vow to practice this skill a lot more... but after some rest.

"Your turn," I tell Bebe. "I think I have energy to learn one more thing today. Maybe."

She smiles impishly. "Have you ever jolted more than one person awake?"

"You mean at the same time?" I ask.

She nods.

"No, I've never tried that. I usually only dreamwalk in one person at a time."

"Well, it can be useful," Bebe says. "Why don't you see if you can manage it with all three of us?"

"All right. But don't resist me. I don't think I can handle all three if you do."

"I bet you can, but I'm game to save it for more advanced lessons," Bebe says. "Now less talking and more jolting."

Taking in a calming breath, I try it.

They're still here.

Is fatigue an emotion? I think it is—so I channel it into my task as Asha suggested.

Boom.

My family is gone.

I jolted them awake.

Bursting with pride, I wake myself up as well.

CHAPTER TWENTY-TWO

I COME to my senses in the waking world.

"Hey," I say, opening my eyes. "I feel much less tired here. Usually, the reverse is true."

"You don't typically attempt to become a single entity with anyone in the waking world." Asha steals a glance at Valerian and winks at me. "Not outside of the bedroom, that is."

I nearly choke.

Valerian grins wickedly, and I hope he isn't comparing our sense of humor, the way Pom did.

"How did it go?" he asks me.

I can't help but smile. "I learned a lot. Can't wait for the next lesson."

"Which will be tomorrow," Bebe says with mock sternness.

"At the soonest," Valerian says, and he seems to mean it.

"Yes, bosses," I say.

A guard walks in, salutes Bebe, and hands her a bundle.

"It's clothes for the three of you." She distributes the bundle into three piles and gives each to Valerian, Maxwell, and me.

I pick up my bundle. The outfit is the same as everyone else's on Soma—silvery and plain.

"Let me show you your rooms," Bebe says and walks out of the medical bay.

Maxwell, Asha, and I happen to glance at Mom at the same exact time, and as our eyes meet above her, our expressions are equally grim.

The machines are exercising her muscles—which looks disturbing, at least to me.

"We'll get her out." I make the words sound like an oath.

They nod, and we follow Bebe.

Maxwell's room is at the beginning of the next corridor, Asha and her family's is across the tower from him, and Valerian and I get the two rooms next to them.

Bebe accompanies me to explain how to use the shower. She then assures me the bedsheets are sterile and self-cleaning, due to a technology that sounds a lot like hygieia.

"Thank you," I say earnestly.

Her eyes gleam with wetness. "It still feels like a dream to have you back here."

"I feel the same." I have a sudden urge to kiss her papery cheek, but the thought of germs stops me. "See you soon."

She leaves, and I test out the shower. Then, feeling nice and clean, I put on my new clothes and step out of the bathroom.

Valerian is waiting for me in the middle of my room. Like me, he looks freshly showered and is wearing the Soma outfit Bebe provided us.

My heartbeat picks up pace, and I suddenly feel warm all over. The silvery material clings to every muscle on his tall, broad-shouldered frame, highlighting the perfection that is his body. And his face... Puck, that face of his is enough to make a girl lose her mind—especially given the dark heat in those ocean-blue eyes.

I fight to get my breathing under control as I close the distance between us. "To what do I owe this pleasure?"

His sensuous mouth quirks. "There was talk of a date.... unless you're too tired."

My pulse spikes further. Holy puck, it's happening. Finally happening. I dampen my lips. "Remember what I said. I don't want any illusions."

His eyes are glued to my mouth. "Not even for a more romantic setting?"

Gathering my courage, I take off my top and toss it on a nearby chair. "I meant you. I want your body and my reactions to it to be real, but you can do what you want with our surroundings."

His gaze roams over my exposed flesh, all but

scorching it with its intensity. "And you're sure you can handle this?"

I bite my lip, trying to keep my mind off all the viruses and bacteria we'll be exchanging. "I think so. But just in case, you can also hide bodily fluids from my sight." And blood, should there be any, with this being my first time and all.

"You got it." Eyes gleaming, he takes his own shirt off.

Oh. My. Estrogen. I've seen him naked before, but knowing this is real, and that I can do what I want to him, makes me feel like my body is going into total meltdown.

I may not be a traditional virgin, having had all kinds of sex in the dream world, but the real thing is brand-new to me, and it's hotter than anything my imagination has conjured up so far.

I channel my dream world self, the one that's completely in control. "Take it all off," I order huskily, and show him what I mean by removing what remains of my clothing.

He obligingly strips, a sexy smirk playing on his lips as he pushes his pants down.

My breath catches in my throat, and Pom's fur turns a deep coral pink on my wrist.

He really *is* gorgeous—all parts of him. Surging forward, I rise on tiptoes just as Valerian dips his head, and we lock lips.

This kiss is better than all the prior ones combined. A tingling electricity spreads through my body, and my knees begin to buckle. His strong hands catch me before I can fall, and in an eyeblink, we're on the bed.

Wow.

He nibbles on my neck. The room around us goes away, replaced with the most majestic nebula in the Cogniverse—and we're flying through it at lightspeed without a spacecraft.

He moves his attention to my clavicle. Double wow. My pulse breaks the sound barrier.

Slowly, torturously, he explores every part of my body until his tongue finds what it must've been searching for.

A thousand wows.

I gasp.

His tongue works relentlessly—until pleasure explodes in my core, and I arch my back.

A star goes supernova in the nebula around us.

His tongue retraces its route back to my neck, and after another nibble, he lifts his head to gaze down at me. "You okay?"

"Continue," I whisper. "Please."

His pupils dilate, and he proceeds, very gently. There's a moment of pain, but soon, it's a distant memory. Instead, a pleasure spreads through me that puts anything I've experienced before—even the high from vampire blood—to shame.

Bigger and more colorful supernovas erupt in the nebula around us, like fireworks, each one coinciding with my orgasms.

He tenses and then relaxes in my arms to one final

supernova explosion, and I hug him tight, though my muscles feel like jelly.

"You should rest," he murmurs, brushing the hair off my forehead, and I nod, smiling up at him.

We turn, getting into a spooning position, and he wraps his arms around me, holding me like he'll never let me go as I close my eyes contentedly and fall into the deepest sleep of my life.

CHAPTER TWENTY-THREE

I WAKE up to the realization that I slept and didn't have a single dream.

Then I remember what had happened just before I fell asleep, and my heart rate picks up. We finally did what I've been yearning for from the moment I met Valerian. But what now? What does it mean? Are we—

My stomach loudly grumbles, and I realize I'm so famished I'd probably risk Earth street food.

Valerian is still spooning me, so I gently wriggle out from under his heavy arm and tiptoe into the bathroom. After a shower, I sneak back into the room and put on my clothes.

Valerian opens one eye. "You heading somewhere?"

"Hungry," I say, something warm and soft filling my chest at the sight of him lying there, all sleep-mussed and sexy.

Yawning, he gets up also and begins to dress.

As I watch, my hunger for food transforms into a

different kind of craving, but before I can act on it, Valerian finishes dressing and says, "Let's go. I'm also famished."

Oh, well. Hopefully we can get right back to it after we eat.

We locate the cafeteria from earlier, and Valerian figures out how to use the dispensing machine to get two silver cubes and a clear container with water. We take a seat at a table, turn the cubes into trays, and I squirt the food from a tube into my mouth without bothering to ask him to make it palatable. After I chase the paste with a few gulps of water, I finally feel like myself again—and questions from earlier resurface.

"Can we talk?" I ask, heat filling my face.

He puts down his tube, a wicked gleam appearing in his eyes. "What's on your mind?"

I reach deep for my courage. "It's about what happened. I just wanted to—"

A loud sound pierces the air, startling the puck out of me.

"Is that you?" I ask Valerian.

Frowning, he shakes his head.

Maxwell rushes into the cafeteria, white as a ghost. "Come with me, now."

He runs out, and we chase him into a room with a wall covered by a floor-to-ceiling screen. With the exception of Mom and my niece, my whole family is here—all staring at the currently blank screen with grim expressions.

"Did something happen to Chloe?" I ask, my mouth going dry.

"We took her to the daycare in this building," Asha says. "She's fine… for now."

Well, that's ominous. So much for going right back to bed activities.

Bebe fiddles with some controls. "I'll show it to you from the beginning."

The screen comes to life, displaying a feed from a drone that seems to be hovering above the entry gate to Soma.

A person steps out of the gate.

It's a large male elf with the fiery eyes of the Overtaken.

CHAPTER TWENTY-FOUR

A TALL GUARD at the gate sends an arc of illusionist energy at the newcomer. The elf looks around in confusion, then dives head first into a nearby moat, breaking his neck in the process.

Before I can let out a relieved breath, another Overtaken steps out of the gate.

And another.

This time, two guards shoot them with illusionist mojo, and the Overtaken start savagely fighting each other.

Another Overtaken emerges from the gate.

And one more. Then two at the same time. And three.

Most of the newcomers are wearing nightwear, and some are armed with things you'd find around a kitchen—tools they cleave and chop each other with, covering the ground with gore.

When there are more of them than there are

illusionist guards, the guards raise their guns and begin shooting.

Another dozen Overtaken leap out of the gate and kick their fallen comrades into the moat.

The guards shoot them too.

More Overtaken emerge.

The guards keep on shooting.

One of the Overtaken hurls a colander at the guards before she gets gunned down.

The moat is beginning to fill up with bodies.

The stream of the Overtaken intensifies to the point where they seem to show up faster than the guards can shoot them. The moat is completely filled up now, and one of the newly arrived Overtaken takes advantage of this and lunges at the closest guard with a knife.

The guard shoots the attacker, but it's too late.

The knife is in his throat.

In my periphery, Bebe grimaces, muttering a name.

Seeing one of their own killed seems to bolster the rest of the guards. With grim efficiency, they gun down the Overtaken killer and his comrades.

But more Overtaken take the place of the fallen ones, and another round of slaughter ensues. Then another.

Bebe rubs the back of her neck. "Do you understand now?"

"The Overtaken came for me," I say, my voice catching in my throat.

"They came for all of us," Bebe says darkly. "I'm

going to fast-forward so we can see what's happening right now."

She fiddles with controls, and the video of the battle speeds up until all I can make out are waves after waves of Overtaken arriving and getting shot down. When the recording resumes playing at normal speed, it's to show the guards putting down yet another score of attackers.

Except the gun of one of the guards doesn't fire when it should—costing him his life.

"Chigi." Bebe's face is a mask of horror. "He'd just joined the guards. What am I going to tell his mother?"

"Why did his gun not shoot?" I ask over a lump in my throat.

"Ran out of charge." Bebe pushes back her white curls. "I was afraid of that."

A man limps into the room.

We all give a start. Given what's happening on the screen, we half-expected him to be one of the Overtaken.

But no. This man's eyes aren't fiery. They do look familiar, though.

"Here are the weapons you requested," the newcomer says and dumps a heap of guns that look just like the ones the guards carry. There are also strange non-shiny swords that clank more like ceramics than metal, and a bunch of wicked-looking machetes.

"Thanks, Idi," Bebe says as I figure out whose eyes Idi's remind me of: Kojo's.

Now that I think about it, they share other features as well.

As if to confirm my theory, the newcomer faces my sister's husband. "Hi, son. Good to see you awake."

Kojo solemnly nods. "I wish we were meeting under better circumstances."

Idi limps over to the only chair in the room and sits with a wince—something is clearly wrong with one of his legs.

On the screen, another guard's gun loses charge, then another.

"We need to do something. Let's take those"—I gesture at the heap of weapons—"and get over there."

Valerian steps in front of me. "It would make more sense to dispatch additional guards."

Bebe rounds on him. "You think that wasn't the very first thing I did?"

She did? That almost makes it sound like she's in c—

A large green figure steps out of the gate on the screen, and my heart rate doubles as I realize it's an orc with fiery eyes. A big specimen that looks like he's been caught in a blast of gamma radiation and now no one likes him when he's angry.

The surviving guards react admirably.

Raising their guns as one, they shoot the orc.

Yes!

Except nothing happens.

Asha gapes at the screen. "Maybe the guns aren't designed for something that big?"

Whatever the reason, the orc rushes the guards,

breaking through them like a linebacker from hell as Bebe gasps in horror.

All the nearby Overtaken use the opportunity to leap at the knocked-down guards.

Four people die.

Bebe looks on the verge of weeping as she recites each of their names under her breath.

A new group of guards emerges from the forest, each armed with two guns and either swords or machetes. They begin to fire at the Overtaken, and once they're done with them, they help their surviving comrades to their feet.

The guards then form a wider perimeter around the gate and gun down the next wave of the Overtaken.

Bebe manipulates the controls again, and a smaller square appears on the screen, showing the Escapist side of Soma—with a green figure of the orc running through it.

"Someone put me under." Kojo lies down on the floor. "If the Escapists don't wake up, he'll kill them."

Asha immediately gestures at him, and I feel him entering REM sleep.

Meanwhile, another orc—a smaller specimen— rushes out of the gate with a bunch of elves, gnomes, and a couple of ubers. The guns don't work on this orc either, but four of the guards attack him with their swords and machetes.

A few bloody slashes later, the orc is dead—and I exhale a breath I didn't realize I was holding.

Meanwhile, the guns of the other guards work just fine on the elves, gnomes, and ubers.

On the smaller screen, the big orc runs at a nearby building, but a guard steps into his path, shooting in desperation.

It's as futile as before.

"Use your illusionist powers," Valerian mutters at the screen. "He's alone."

The guard must realize the same thing. An arc of energy hits the orc on the head, halting him in his tracks.

The orc looks around in confusion. Then, seemingly recovering, he runs right into the nearby wall, bloodying his forehead.

He does this over and over, until he drops to the floor.

I guess that's the silver lining of the fact that the Overtaken feel no pain. They can clobber themselves like that.

Meanwhile, on the larger section of the screen, another big orc jumps out of the gate. Then another. When there are four of them, they rush the guards.

Two orcs get chopped into pieces with the swords, but two make it through.

Again, they run for the Escapist side of Soma, where the guard who just defeated their big cousin bravely faces them.

Jaw clenched tight, he shoots them with his mojo.

Nothing happens.

"His powers won't work against the two," Valerian says despairingly.

Realizing the same thing, the guard flings his useless gun at the nearest orc's head.

It doesn't slow his onslaught in the least.

Grabbing the guard by his throat, the orc squeezes his green fingers.

"Fight, Jahi!" Bebe yells, her eyes glued to the small screen.

But Jahi's kicks make no impact on his bulky attacker, and he slumps into a dead heap at the orcs' feet.

Jumping over Jahi's body, the orcs run into the building, and an ashen Bebe turns the controls again, switching the camera view to the inside.

Huge eyes shining like flames, the orcs break into the first apartment.

There's a family inside—a mother, father, and two children—hooked up to the machines the way my twin was.

I want to look away, but something forces me to keep on watching.

At my side, Asha is weeping quietly, her hand covering her mouth.

One by one, the orcs choke the parents, then the children.

"Put me under," Asha says frantically, stretching out on the floor. "I need to see what's taking Kojo so long."

I move to do it, but Maxwell gets to her first, swiftly sending her into REM sleep.

On the bigger screen, the guards put down two more waves of the Overtaken.

Bebe rounds on Idi. "We need to warn my people. The guards may not be able to contain this."

He nods tersely as I stare at my grandmother. "Bebe, are you Soma's leader?"

She gives me a distracted glance. "I'm the Elder. Idi here is my second-in-command."

Aha. That's why she was able to override security cameras willy-nilly. But there's no time to dwell on it because a group of naked Overtaken exit the gate on the screen.

In a flash, they turn into wolves and leap at the guards.

Idi thrusts a microphone-like device into Bebe's hands.

Her spine turns ramrod straight as she lifts the device to her mouth. "Citizens of Soma." Her voice booms out of the ceiling in the room—and presumably everywhere. "We are under attack."

I stop paying attention to her as the fight on the screen escalates.

Though the guns do work on the werewolves, the canine Overtaken are just too fast. In an eyeblink, ten guards are ripped into shreds.

At the sight of the massacre, tears stream down Bebe's face, but her voice doesn't waver as she explains the situation to the rest of Soma.

The remaining guards on the screen finally contain

the werewolves, but at a cost. Their perimeter is noticeably sparser.

"—Soma shall prevail," I catch Bebe saying before she hands the microphone back to Idi.

Asha suddenly sits up, cursing—and Kojo jackknifes to his feet, talking over her.

"Speak one at a time," Bebe orders. "What happened?"

Kojo moderates his tone. "They refused to believe us. They won't wake up."

"More like won't face reality," Asha says, jumping to her feet. "Even to save their lives."

Bebe looks like she's aged another couple of years during that exchange. "So be it. The guards will do the best they can for them."

As if to illustrate, two guards armed with swords attack the orcs on the smaller screen.

Kojo and Asha stare at the larger screen with despair and fury.

One of the Overtaken that's not an orc remains standing when a guard shoots him. Two more guards aim at him, but also fail to bring him down.

A female guard dives out of the perimeter, slashing her sword at the stubborn invader. The blade enters the Overtaken's shoulder—but comes out on the other side as if he were made of vapor.

"A chort," I say, watching in horror. "They can phase."

The female guard must realize this too, because she retreats. Only it's too late. The chort kills her with a single touch, then grabs her sword and tosses it to the next person who steps out of the gate.

I gawk at the newcomer.

Those symmetrical masculine features and strong dark eyebrows are unmistakable.

It's Rattie—the person who was secretly the Nutcracker, a dreamwalker I vanquished in the dream world and thus made homicidally insane.

Right now, his eyes are filled with fire, which means that instead of his damaged mind, he's being controlled by Phobetor's no less dangerous intelligence.

Valerian narrows his eyes at the screen. "So this is where he went. I hope the guards get him."

The guards do not. They're too busy with the chort.

Asha curses again as a giant jumps out of the gate.

At first, I think it's Colton, but no. This one is female, and she's at least two heads taller.

The guards not too busy with the chort shoot at her. Just like with the orcs, the guns don't seem to work due to the female giant's size. With steps that shake the forest around them, she lumbers toward the guards nearest her.

Rattie hangs back, as do all the regular-sized Overtaken as they stream in through the gate.

Before the giant gets to her destination, the guards in her way drop their guns and ready their swords. She smashes into them without any attempt at self-preservation. Ignoring the sword a brave guard sticks into her left thigh, she grabs him and uses him like a club to bash the others.

A couple of swings later, a dozen guards are on the ground.

Rattie and a small army of the Overtaken must've been waiting for just this opening. Without bothering to finish off the downed guards, they vault over them and launch into a sprint.

When I realize which way they're headed, ice fills my stomach.

They're running to our side of Soma.

CHAPTER TWENTY-FIVE

"WHAT DO WE DO?" Idi gasps out.

"Make a stand." Bebe rushes to the nearby table and takes out small earplug-like devices.

Idi limps over to the weapon pile, but Bebe grabs his shoulder. "We need someone to stay back and update us on the developing situation."

She thrusts an earpiece into Asha's hand, and my sister shoves it into her ear, then grabs a gun and a sword.

Kojo frowns at the weapons in his wife's hands. "Why don't you stay with Idi?"

There's a ferocious gleam in Asha's eyes. "My child is in this building. The only way the Overtaken are getting in is over my dead body."

Mine too.

I snatch up an earpiece for myself, then stride over to the weapon pile and pick up a gun and a sword.

Valerian grabs my wrist. "I want you to stay with Idi."

I twist out of his hold. "I'm going to protect my family."

He stares at me for a tense second, then sighs. "I had to try."

He takes up weapons of his own, and Bebe, Maxwell, and Kojo do the same.

With grim determination, we sprint out of the building.

Once outside, I discover we're not the only ones who've gotten this idea. A group of armed people are already here, as well as more teams by the entrances of the other buildings nearby.

Bebe's rousing speech must be the cause.

"We need to form a tactical formation," Bebe says and orders us to stand like a firing squad, backs to the building and guns pointed at the edge of the forest.

I end up on the rightmost end of the line, with Bebe on my left, Asha on her left, then Valerian, then Kojo, then Maxwell, then people whose names I don't know.

A second later, a pair of elves dash out of the forest —a male and a female, both dressed in sleepwear, as most Overtaken are.

"Illusions!" Bebe shouts.

Valerian and one of the other defenders shoot the Overtaken with arcs of energy.

The elves freeze. Then the female attacks the male, tearing out his hair. He smashes a fist at her face, shattering her nose. She gouges out his left eye—which is when another pair of Overtaken appear out of the forest.

An uber and a dwarf.

"We don't have four illusionists," Bebe shouts. "Fire on my command!"

The elves stop fighting. Now that the Overtaken outnumber the illusionists, Phobetor can't be fooled.

The four race at us, the gravely injured elves oblivious to pain.

When they're fifteen feet away, Bebe hollers for us to fire.

I shoot the rightmost Overtaken—the dwarf.

He collapses, tripping one of the wounded elves in the process.

I shoot the downed elf as my allies take care of the rest.

"The giant is finally dead," Idi's voice says triumphantly in my ear. "Oh, wait, now there's an orc."

"Give us tactically critical information only," Bebe barks into her earpiece. "Can't afford to be distracted."

"Understood," Idi replies.

Another group of Overtaken—all naked—streak out of the forest, so we gun them down. An even larger group barrels out next, but we destroy them too. This pattern repeats until my trigger finger is cramping from all the squeezing.

A pair of dwarves fly out of the forest like birds.

I resist the temptation to rub my eyes.

It soon becomes clear that they're not actually

flying. More like hovering ten feet off the ground. Under them is another motley crew of Overtaken.

They all charge at us.

"There's a telekinetic in that group." Idi's voice is somber. "He's caused chaos back at the gate and is now causing the dwarves to float."

Not just float. Whoever the telekinetic is, he catapults the dwarves at us.

I fire upward—as does everyone else.

A lifeless dwarf whooshes over my head and smashes into the ground. Another one slams into one of the men in the middle of our formation, knocking him off his feet.

"Fire!" Bebe yells.

My finger spasms over the trigger. The others shoot as well. Five Overtaken collapse, but clearly not the telekinetic—who must be the one launching the limp bodies of our enemies toward us.

I sidestep, and an elf crashes into the wall behind me.

To my left, Bebe ducks to avoid a dwarf. So do Asha, Kojo, and Maxwell.

I shoot at the Overtaken again—dropping an uber.

There's a sudden telekinetic jerk on my gun.

Oh, puck. I grip the handle as if our lives depend on it, since they do. The force of the next pull drags me forward, my feet skidding on the grass.

Nope. I'm not giving up my gun.

The handle begins to jerk up and down, lifting me off the ground, then smashing me back down.

I dig into the grass with my heels and hold on for dear life. I'd shoot too, but aiming in this situation is impossible. I could hit myself or my allies.

"Use your sword!" Bebe shouts. "We can't allow them to get that gun."

Puck, she's right.

Unclenching my fingers, I slice with the ceramic sword. There's a screech as the cleaved-in-half gun careens toward the Overtaken.

Pivoting, I dash back to rejoin my squad, but the telekinetic has already moved on to the next victim.

Maxwell gets dragged forward by his gun. He copies my earlier maneuver by slashing his gun in two before he lets the telekinetic have it.

If this keeps up, we'll be defenseless.

Kojo is pulled out of the ranks next, but by his sword instead of his gun. He releases the hilt, and the weapon whooshes over the heads of the Overtaken and disappears into the forest.

Well, at least the telekinetic didn't take it.

Valerian aims carefully at someone behind me and pulls the trigger. The others do the same. Reaching my spot in the formation, I spin around to see what they've accomplished.

All the Overtaken are now down. The telekinetic shouldn't be bothering us anymore.

I feel a spurt of hope, but in the next moment, Rattie steps out of the forest, a sword in each hand.

Unbelievable. How did I manage to forget about him?

The situation quickly worsens. Hundreds more attackers follow Rattie, and instead of running for us right away, as the others have done, they stay near the forest, gathering forces.

"Shoot!" Bebe orders.

Everyone on our squad fires, but they only get a couple of Overtaken at this distance.

As the enemies gather, I miss my gun more and more. I'm also increasingly concerned about the guns running out of charge.

The Overtaken assemble for a few more seconds, oblivious to the loss of the ones we've taken out. Then, as one, they begin their assault in a massive horde.

Our makeshift troops fire, over and over. The Overtaken fall, but their comrades simply vault over their bodies and keep on coming.

And it's bad.

Halfway to us, a whopping ninety percent of the Overtaken are still in the running.

When they're forty feet away, our guns make a bigger impact, but there are still at least two dozen Overtaken barreling toward us, with Rattie in the lead. His eyes darts between me and Asha before finally settling on me.

Everyone fires desperately.

They miss Rattie and a few others, who are almost upon us.

"Prepare for close-quarters combat!" Bebe shouts needlessly.

I grip my sword handle until my knuckles whiten.

When he's about ten feet away, Rattie shouts, "Die!" and hurls one of his swords at me.

There's a blur of movement.

No.

Not this.

I gape at Bebe.

The sword meant for me is protruding from her stomach.

CHAPTER TWENTY-SIX

WHEEZING, my grandmother slumps.

Though she's clutching the grievous wound with both hands, it doesn't stop the gushing of her blood.

My heartbeat pounds deafeningly in my ears. Through the haze of shock and fear, I realize two things.

First, Bebe jumped in the path of the flying sword to save my life.

Second, and more importantly, Rattie is almost here, so unless I act this very instant, Bebe's sacrifice will have been for naught.

Shaking off the haze, I leap over Bebe, putting myself between her and Rattie. Out of the corner of my eye, I see the Overtaken reach the rest of my family and allies. In the span of an eyeblink, Valerian beheads an elf, and Kojo shoots an uber.

Rattie lunges at me with the sword.

I dodge, but his blade nicks my upper arm. The pain

is sharp and stinging, but I recover quickly and parry his next hit.

He slashes at me again.

I block instinctively, and sparks fly where our two ceramic-like blades clash.

We end up in a lock with the swords crisscrossed in a horizontal position.

I push against the clinch to try to knock him off balance.

He doesn't budge.

When he does the same to me, I somehow manage to stand firm, feet rooted to the ground. Even with him being waif thin, as a guy, he has the advantage of strength, but I have desperation on my side.

Still, with me bleeding, I won't last long and he knows it.

I give him my best death glare. It's probably my overactive imagination, but I feel like I see Phobetor's face deep in those fiery depths. A sadistic part of me I didn't realize existed wants to reach into those eyes and choke the god of nightmares with my bare hands for hurting Bebe.

Rattie pushes with renewed force, an ugly expression contorting his handsome features.

I push back, matching his strength.

"Tick-tock," he sneers. "Your grandmother is bleeding out, like a stuck mooft. And so are you."

I'm so angry I feel like my own eyes might burst into flames.

Baring my teeth like an animal, I growl, "If she

dies, I will hunt you down to the ends of the dream world. God or not, I will end you." Leveraging my fury, I strain my quivering triceps to shove again with my sword—and at the same time, I kick his shin, hard.

Though there's no sign of pain on his face, he does lose his balance for a second—which is all I need to open a deep cut in his shoulder.

Is that concern in those fiery eyes? Can't be. Phobetor doesn't care about losing this one body.

His next thrust is at my neck.

I parry, then hack and slash at him viciously, eager to draw more blood.

He counters every slice.

I block his strikes as well, but my muscles are growing tired, and the loss of blood is making me woozy.

Rattie's shoulder wound is bleeding too, but I doubt it'll mess with his concentration.

He lunges at me again, leaving a gash in my side.

Puck.

I need to win and soon.

Somehow.

The next round of attacks is brutal, but I'm beginning to notice something.

There's a pattern to Phobetor's movements.

A pattern I can exploit.

I block and dodge the next couple of strikes and wait for my moment. If I'm right, there will be an opening soon.

There. I stab his thigh as he prepares for the thrust part of his pattern.

Again, there's no sign of pain on his face, but there's more anger there. More importantly, his footwork is now compromised, so I must've done some real damage.

Is he going to continue the pattern? It might be all he knows.

And he does keep going in the same vein. Except when I exploit it again, I miss his neck and only nick his ear.

Puck.

His eyes narrow and the fire disappears from them, replaced by madness.

Double puck.

Without Phobetor's control, Rattie has reverted to what he's become after I killed him in the dream world —a homicidal maniac.

I attack, hoping I catch him off guard.

Nope.

He blocks, and with an animalistic roar, he swings the sword wildly. I barely dodge the attack, and the onslaught that follows. In theory, Rattie is vulnerable to illusion powers once more, but I don't dare distract Valerian for that. Instead, I attempt to push my opponent into REM sleep, figuring that will bring Phobetor back in the worst case, or make Rattie sleep in the best case.

It doesn't work. Either he's in a strange dream-like

state already, or I have too much adrenaline to work my powers.

Doing my best to ignore the weakness and cold brought about by the blood loss, I attack him, then defend myself as I study his repertoire of movements.

Aha. Rattie's attacks begin to remind me of the time I fought him in his Nutcracker guise in the dream world, but remixed through insanity. Going on a hunch, I raise the sword above my head and slice down with all my strength.

He blocks just in time, and a flash of sparks later, we're in a carbon copy of our prior crisscrossed sword lock. Except this time, things are different. Insane or not, he's more able to feel pain than Phobetor—so I smash my knee into his groin.

Rattie screams like a wounded boar.

I shove harder, and his own sword slices his face.

His eyes widen, and fire returns to them—but too late.

I pierce his chest, my blade penetrating breastbone and entering his heart.

CHAPTER TWENTY-SEVEN

RATTIE'S BODY COLLAPSES, eyes lifeless.

Panting, I whirl around and scan the rest of the battlefield.

An Overtaken has his hands wrapped around Asha's throat. My sister's eyes are wild with panic, but she's struggling valiantly.

I dash over there and chop off the enemy's hands at the wrists. Freed, Asha gasps for air and shoots the crippled Overtaken in the head at the same time.

Then we join forces and help Valerian with the uber he's been fighting.

Next, we look over to where Maxwell and Kojo are fighting a werewolf in animal form. Both dreamwalkers have gashes from claws and teeth, and are bleeding profusely.

Asha and Valerian shoot the werewolf in the head at the same exact time.

The beast collapses.

We help everyone else next, dispatching the rest of the Overtaken one by one.

"Bebe," I pant when the last of the enemies is no more.

Tossing our weapons aside, Asha and I rush over to her and kneel on either side.

Her face ashen, Bebe lies in a pool of blood. Her breath is shallow, coming out in pained gurgles.

"I couldn't allow you to be killed," she chokes out, her gray eyes glued to my face.

"Hush," I whisper raggedly. "Save your strength."

"Take her to the medical bay," Valerian says urgently, coming to kneel at my side. "Kojo, Maxwell, and Asha can help you make sure she isn't jostled. Once she's safe, you all should patch yourselves up as well."

I throw a frantic glance at the forest. "What if there's another attack?"

As if to confirm my fears, an Overtaken elf steps out, then an uber.

"We'll handle them," Valerian says and tosses Asha's gun to a dreamwalker who needs it. "Go."

With a heavy heart, I work with the others to carefully lift Bebe.

As we step into the building, her breaths grow more labored, and her gaze struggles to focus on Asha and me.

We hurry as gently as we can, leaving a trail of Bebe's blood behind us.

Midway to the medical bay, the sound of her strained breaths stops.

Ice coats my chest, and my throat feels like it's being squeezed in a brutal fist. "Please hang on," I whisper to my grandmother. "Please, please, just hang on."

The rest of the way is a blur.

Once inside the sterile room of the bay, we lay Bebe's frail body on a gurney.

A woman wearing all white dashes over. "I'm the doctor on duty," she says quickly, already feeling for my grandmother's pulse.

Her face goes carefully blank, and she does several more checks as I watch, Pom's fur the dullest gray it's ever been.

I know what she's about to tell us before she turns to face us, pain and regret gleaming in her eyes. Even so, I need her to spell it out because a part of me refuses to believe it. Doesn't want to believe it.

"I'm sorry." The doctor's voice wavers. "She's gone. The sword went straight through—"

I don't hear the rest.

My knees give out, and I sink to the floor. On the other side of the gurney, Asha does the same, her face —a mirror image of mine—a mask of anguish.

I can't process this, can't deal with the grief that feels like a giant sitting on my chest. Numbly, I watch as Kojo crouches next to Asha and gathers her into his embrace.

She starts to cry.

I wish I could as well, but I barely knew my grandmother—and that's what hurts the most. It's all the years we didn't get to spend together, all the hugs that were never given, all the wisdom I'll never learn from her.

The doctor shakes off her own grief and begins applying first aid to everyone as Maxwell approaches me uncertainly.

"Bailey," he says hoarsely. "Are you okay?"

I nod. What else can I say? Everyone here has way more reason to be grieving than I do.

I've never felt more like an outsider in my life than I do in this moment, surrounded by family I don't remember and don't really know.

Eyes somber, my father squeezes my shoulder, and I draw in a steadying breath, shoving down that hollow, choking feeling. "Valerian," I say thickly. "He's out there. We have to help him."

With his life on the line and Soma on the brink of destruction, I can't just sit and wallow.

Maxwell frowns. "You're injured. He can—"

Idi clears his throat in the earpiece, reminding me the device is still in my ear. "An Overtaken necromancer has just arrived at the gate. He's resurrecting the fallen on both sides. I'm sending the rest of the guards down there. It's our only chance."

The faces of everyone around me reflect the same despair I'm feeling.

A necromancer is bad news. Horrific news.

I need to do something. *We* need to do something. But what?

"I'm going to take her to the morgue," the doctor says somberly, and starts wheeling the gurney out.

No one stops her, though a part of me wants to.

"This is all my fault." The words escape my mouth as if of their own accord. "Phobetor is after me. If I'd stayed away from Soma, Bebe would still be alive."

Asha stops crying and gives me an incredulous look. "Two as One, remember?" she says with a hiccup. "He wants me just as much as he wants you."

Maxwell nods grimly. "Asha's right. This attack was carefully planned. He wouldn't have had time to set it up *after* we arrived. If anything, your presence saved some lives."

I shake my head, my throat tight again. "It was me she jumped to protect."

"And I'm sure she'd do it all over again, as would I," Maxwell says. "And it wasn't because of the damned prophecy. She loved you and couldn't let you die."

The prophecy. How could I have forgotten about that?

A true hero destined to destroy an evil wouldn't have forgotten. If we needed more proof that I'm not it, here it is.

Puck that.

My spine straightens, a burst of anger chasing away the hollow grief and guilt.

I don't care if the prophecy is about me, or if it's even true.

Things are much simpler now.

Bebe is dead, and I made Phobetor a promise about this exact outcome—and as the god of nightmares is my witness, I will keep my promise.

I will either destroy him or die trying.

The pressure in my throat eases a smidge, and a dark smile crosses my lips, even as the scope of what I plan to undertake sends tendrils of fear throughout my body.

I catch my sister's gaze.

They say twins can read each other's minds—and I feel it in this moment.

I know she's arrived at a conclusion similar to mine.

I leap to my feet. "There's a way to save everyone on Soma. A way that doesn't require the use of swords and guns. Not real ones, anyway."

Asha also jumps to her feet, the determined expression on her face mirroring mine. "Yes. We take the fight to Phobetor."

"We kill him in the dream world," we say in unison.

CHAPTER TWENTY-EIGHT

MAXWELL DRAWS BACK, staring at us in disbelief. "You're not ready. You need months of training first. If—"

"We don't have a choice." I begin to pace. "A necromancer is a formidable foe, and who knows what other surprises await us in the real world."

Kojo catches my sister's wrist. "You haven't figured out the Two as One technique."

"We'll just have to do without it," Asha says. "Our parents didn't have a technique, and they took him on."

"And got Overtaken." Maxwell darts a glance at Mom's comatose body. "You need to do better than we did."

I stop. "We *are* doing this. From here on out, we only talk logistics."

Maxwell opens his mouth, then closes it, a defeated expression stealing over his face. "We need allies. Dreamwalkers and illusionists ideally, but any

Cognizant could help—especially if they have powers."

"Why?" Asha asks. "If it's the dream world..."

Maxwell winces. "Phobetor always has an army of creatures with him." He looks at me. "Subdream monsters, you call them."

That makes sense, and my father's idea of bringing in allies could help face such an army. Someone comfortable with their powers can use them in the dream world as a form of lucid dreaming. A dreamwalker would be able to annul their powers, of course, but I don't think subdream creatures would have that power.

The best part is, those who aren't dreamwalkers have one huge advantage in a fight like this: If they get killed, they'll simply wake up, as if from a nightmare.

The doctor comes back in, but we ignore her.

Kojo doesn't look happy as he says, "Let me speak with the Escapists again. Maybe they'll—"

"It's worth a shot," Asha says. "But first, I have a question. How do we actually find Phobetor in the dream world?"

"Me." Maxwell's eyes gleam. "I'm always fighting him off. If I give up that fight, you'll face him. When your mother and I—"

"Hold on." Kojo looks at Maxwell as if he's grown a set of antlers. "Won't you become one of the Overtaken in the process?"

Maxwell's expression is pained. "I should be tied down. In fact, all of us should be. Just in case..."

Asha turns to the doctor and explains the part of the conversation the woman missed. Then she asks, "Do you have something we can use to restrain ourselves?"

"The Overtaken aren't a new problem," the doctor says and sprints over to a cabinet. She returns with thick, bandage-like ropes that she attaches to special grooves in the four nearby gurneys.

She then gestures for us to lie down.

Reluctantly, I stretch out on a gurney, and the others do the same.

"Ready?" the doctor asks.

Half-hearted agreements all around.

She restrains us.

No one brings up an obvious point. If an Overtaken —even a weak one—gets past Valerian and the others, we're toast.

"Now," Maxwell says, pulling me out of my dark thoughts. "I'll put Asha under, and she'll bring the rest of us in from the inside."

"I'm ready," Asha says.

I can feel her go into REM sleep, followed by Maxwell and Kojo.

How will it feel when she drags me in like that? Maybe like anesthesia or—

———

I FIND myself standing on a gelatinous surface inside a canyon of chocolate mountains, with the sky above reminiscent of cotton candy.

Is this another Escapist Domain? Maybe Food or Dessert?

My family are already here, so I don't waste time asking about the environment.

"A good place to gather all the forces," Maxwell says, gesturing at the delicious landscape.

As if summoned by those words, Pom appears in the middle of our gathering, his fur a light shade of orange. "What's going on?" He looks at Kojo curiously. "Who's that?"

Speaking fast, I explain that introductions will have to wait for later because we're in a life-and-death situation and about to face the god of nightmares himself.

As I speak, Pom's fur turns darker and his ears take on a beet hue. "That sounds beyond scary."

I pet the top of his head. "We can do this without you. In fact, it might make it easier for me if I don't have to worry about you getting hurt."

He shakes his head, his ears turning teal. "I want to help."

"Fair enough. How about I'll mentally call for you if I need you? That way, you can gather your courage in the meanwhile."

Pom turns a dark purple and gives me a military salute with his paw. "You got it." He performs his best Cheshire Cat disappearance.

"I'm off to recruit the Escapists," Kojo says and disappears as well, without fanfare in his case.

"What about me?" Asha asks. "I don't really know anyone that Kojo doesn't."

"Remember the dream constructs from my earlier lesson?" our father asks.

Asha's eyes brighten. "I did want to experiment with that."

A unicorn with humanoid arms appears in the distance and shouts something to Asha.

"A character from the Escapist myths," she explains. "Let me make more."

Different people and creatures begin to show up, along with a version of Kojo that looks more noble and buff than the real thing.

"We'll do this too," Maxwell says to me. "But after we bring in the real people, since they need to be briefed."

I nod, already thinking along the same lines. "This is where your status as an ambassador between worlds could pay off. You must've gotten to know many powerful Cognizant."

Asha quirks an eyebrow, and I explain how Icelus used Rattie to coordinate between worlds, and how Maxwell was chosen to do something similar for the good guys.

"The problem is that I don't know those powerful Cognizant too well," Maxwell says. "I hope I'm convincing enough to get them to join our dream battle."

"I believe in you," I say.

"Thanks." He smiles and disappears.

"Later," I tell Asha and take myself to my tower of sleepers.

Looking around, I debate my first choice of an ally.

A lot of the people from New York are asleep right now. It must be nighttime in that part of Earth. Sadly, some Earth Cognizant with the best powers—like Nina, Kit, Colton, and Chester—are Overtaken and therefore not available.

On the bright side, Ariel is here, and so are Rowan and most of the rest of the New York Council—people who are presumably grateful to me for finding a murderer in their midst.

I decide to start with Rowan, figuring it would be fitting to get help from a necromancer in the dream battle while another necromancer threatens us in the real world.

The question is whether Rowan will be able to use her power here.

Only one way to find out.

I jump into Rowan's dreams.

———

ROWAN IS SITTING in front of a glass-covered display with a variety of spiders, flies, and other creepy-crawlers inside. Lifting the glass, she starts pinning a cockroach into an empty slot.

Gross. Those things live in garbage and spread all

the worst germs of Earth. I wouldn't touch one even in the dream world.

Pointedly clearing my throat, I wave to get Rowan's attention.

She drops both the pin and the cockroach and rubs her eyes—without first sanitizing her hands.

Wrinkling my nose, I make the critters disappear. "I didn't realize you were an entomologist. Unless this is a creepy hobby?"

"Sleeping beauty," Rowan exclaims, grinning. "Am I dreaming you, or are you dreaming me?"

I return her smile. "How would you be conscious of yourself if I were dreaming you?"

She shrugs. "Your awesome power?"

"I'm actually in a rush," I say and rattle out what I want and why.

Her eyes grow ever wider as I go on.

"So," I say in conclusion. "Will you help us?"

"I guess," she says. "Especially if you can tell me how I'm supposed to use necromancy in my dreams."

I create zombies for her, specifically her macabre entourage from Necronia, masks and all. The zombies begin to move around in strange patterns, and Rowan grins at this like only a necromancer would.

"It works just like if I were awake," she explains. "So cool. I've already grown to miss this."

Miss it? She must not be allowed to use her powers on Earth. I want to ask her, but there's no time. The fates of Valerian and all of Soma are on the line.

"Let me take you to our meeting place," I say. "Once

there, do your best to summon even more corpses. My sister can help you with it."

"Your sister?" she and her zombies ask at the same time.

Instead of answering, I take us to the yummy-looking canyon and quickly introduce her to Asha.

"This is another way you can help us," I tell my twin as I examine the thousands of dream constructs she's already manifested. "How about I bring people here, and you explain what's what to them?"

She grins mischievously. "I could even pretend to be you to make it quicker."

"Suit yourself," I say and return to the tower of sleepers.

After a second of deliberation, I decide to dreamwalk in Ariel next.

I find her dreaming about chopping off vampire heads with her gate sword. I watch for a second, worried that without my supervision, she'll succumb to the temptation to drink vampire blood.

Nope. She ignores the blood completely. This must be about violence, which, though a little disturbing, is still healthier than the addictive alternative.

Revealing my presence to her, I deliver her to my sister for explanations.

The next person I recruit is Vickie, the siren from the New York Council.

"What about Felix?" Ariel asks when she sees me show up with the siren. "I think he'd want to help."

"I didn't see him sleeping," I say.

Ariel chuckles. "He had his girlfriend over. I bet there's a pillow fight going on right this moment."

"You can put your friend into REM sleep from here," Asha says. "Remember what I taught you?"

"He's on another world," I say. "There's no way I—"

"You can," Asha says. "Use your emotions."

My emotions are still in such turmoil I don't know which one I should utilize. Settling on fear, I close my eyes and picture Felix in every detail, from his unibrow to his thin, lanky frame.

"Here goes," I mutter and will Felix into REM sleep.

"What the hell?" Felix's voice is panicked. "Where am I?"

I open my eyes and grin at him. "I drew you into the dream world with my mighty powers."

He looks at our surroundings, then at some of the fantastical constructs Asha created, then at her face. "Either I'm crazy, or this is a dream."

"Or both," Ariel says with a grin.

Felix suddenly blushes like a maiden. "What happened to my body in the real world?"

"It's asleep," I reply.

Even his ears redden now. "Any chance you can jolt me awake so I can explain this to my date? Afterward, you can bring me right back."

I nod toward Asha. "My sister will help you. She'll also explain what we're doing and help you recreate your robot suit."

Without waiting for anyone to object, I return to the tower of sleepers and dreamwalk in another member of the New York Council. Then another—until I get them all in the chocolate canyon, practicing their powers.

From there, I start pulling in people more indiscriminately, even going as far as asking some of my patients to help out.

On a hunch, I leap into the dreams of Napoleon, the lutin who's my Gomorran underworld connection. He helped us during the Icelus investigation.

As often happens in his dreams, instead of looking like the little red devil that's his awake form, he's in the guise of a short man wearing a bicorne. And like the last time I was in his dreams, he's walking on a beach on an island called Elba.

"You're in luck," I say without preamble. "You get to help with a battle that might put the best of Earth military history to shame."

Battles are a fetish of his, so much so he forced me to recreate them in his dreams as a form of payment.

Napoleon's deep-set gray-blue eyes gleam with avarice, and I take him to our scrumptious place of gathering.

He whistles when he spots all the people already here.

"Is this all of your army?" he asks with his signature French accent.

"Only the start of it," I say. "More is coming." Hopefully.

"Who's the foe?" he asks.

"My sister will explain," I say and introduce them.

"Wait, this is Napoleon?" Ariel asks when she overhears the introduction. "Isn't he supposed to be smaller and redder?"

Felix—who has on his robot suit—lifts his face plate. "More importantly, why has Mr. Nain Rouge made himself look like *the* Napoleon?"

"I am *the* Napoleon," the lutin says. "Now tell me about the opposing army. *Hâte.*"

I leave Asha to explain everything, and go on to recruit whoever I can.

When I get back, Maxwell and Kojo are still off recruiting, so I work on my own army of dream constructs, starting with versions of some of the people already here, including Felix and Ariel. Next, I manifest Valerian, hoping the entire time the real one is okay. Itzel is constructed next; with her being a gnome, I couldn't push her into REM sleep.

After this, I create dream versions of our Necronia travel companions, both the ones who are currently Overtaken—like Kit, Colton, Nina, and Chester—and the departed, a.k.a. Fabian, Edith, and Stanislav.

That team joins the conversation with Dream Felix and Dream Ariel, and I work on the copies of my patients and celebrities, starting with Joygasm Troglodyte, Dracula, Robin Hood, Frankenstein, Zorro, and Tarzan. I continue until every comic book hero and god I know is present, ending with Zeus.

"Hey now, where's Batman?" Ariel demands. "How could you skip the best hero in the history of fiction?"

"Forget him, he has no powers. Where is Neo?"

Felix asks indignantly. "Dream world is close enough to the Matrix that—"

"It has to be a character I'm familiar with," I reply.

"Batman is the best," Ariel says.

"No, Neo is," Felix retorts.

I open my mouth to shut them up when Maxwell shows up with an army larger than mine and Asha's combined. He must've gathered his team elsewhere and teleported them all at once—a feat I'll have to attempt someday.

"Maybe it's for the best that we're challenging Phobetor after all," he says. "The situation all around the Cogniverse is dire. The Overtaken are attacking people at random now. Trillions are dying. Countless Cognizant fail to wake up from nightmares. On some worlds, even humans are—"

Kojo suddenly appears, and with him, yet another army.

All the Escapists have the infinity halos above their heads like Asha's family did when I first met them, and some of their faces are identical to Asha's dream constructs, which makes sense since she's lived in that community most of her life.

"You came," Asha exclaims, looking at them excitedly. "Thank you."

"Your husband is persistent," says an Escapist woman with noble features.

"That he is," my sister confirms with a smile.

"What now?" I ask Maxwell.

He averts his gaze. "I'll make it so that Phobetor and his minions appear."

I frown. "What about the part where you sacrifice yourself to our enemy?"

"It will be temporary," Maxwell says. "Once you win, I'll be myself again."

"If," Felix mutters, and Ariel gives him a glare.

"We'll make sure that we do." I pat Felix's robot suit on the back. "Now let's delve into the nitty-gritty of our strategy."

CHAPTER TWENTY-NINE

EVERYONE'S MOOD seems to lift, so I must've said the right thing. Napoleon jauntily strides over, as do Asha, Kojo, Ariel, Felix, Rowan, the Council members from the different worlds, and a few leaders from the Escapist horde.

Maxwell gestures at a nearby chocolate mountain, and it melts away, replaced by a football-field-sized structure that looks like the biggest snow globe in history. Inside it is the familiar subdream sky that looks to be made from magma, with black water below it.

"Here is his army—at least as much of it as we experienced before he took us over," Maxwell says and populates the subdream simulation with millions of monsters. Some are those I've encountered, but many are new to me, though just as horrific.

"The cavalry," Napoleon says, nodding at the army of warthog-spider mounts and their tentacled naked mole rat riders. "And that's air support." He points at the cloud of skeletal turkey vultures and other flying abominations that fill the air between the sky and the ocean. "Lots of infantry." He gestures at the various beasts, among which I recognize the monstrous versions of tardigrades, spiral worms, ants, nail-sword critters, and anglers.

"All formidable," Maxwell says grimly. "Yet all of them combined don't come close to the threat that is Phobetor." He makes the dreaded figure appear behind the troops as everyone stares in horror. "If a dreamwalker gets beyond this point"—he draws a line halfway through the battlefield—"they risk becoming one of the Overtaken. From there, the closer to Phobetor, the higher the risk."

Napoleon scratches his chin. "What are the capabilities of our troops?"

Maxwell points at the dream constructs. "They're the weakest—merely extensions of the dreamwalker who created them."

"Cannon fodder." Napoleon's eyes narrow. "Can you make more?"

In answer, countless more dream constructs show up, all a lot like Asha's, which means it's the work of the Escapists.

"What about me and the other dreamers?" Napoleon asks. "What are our capabilities?"

Asha tears her gaze away from Phobetor and faces Napoleon. "Unless you're familiar with lucid dreaming techniques, your powers will roughly match those you have in the real world."

"That's if you don't get on Phobetor's radar," Maxwell says. "If you do, you'll die instantly—or be turned into an Overtaken, depending on his whim. Either way, you'll be out of the battle."

"You will wake up, though, if you die," Asha chimes in before anyone panics. "Like from a nightmare."

"Exactly," Maxwell says. "Death here means rude awakening for anyone who isn't a dreamwalker. But for us, it's insanity—assuming we don't turn into the Overtaken. Understand?"

Everyone solemnly nods.

"What about those?" Napoleon wrinkles his nose at Rowan's masked zombies.

"Part of my power," Rowan says. "I'm a necromancer."

"Zombies." Napoleon examines Rowan with keen interest. "Even better cannon fodder. Can we bolster their numbers too?"

The zombie army grows exponentially in an eyeblink.

Wow. Escapists are very good at this dreamwalking business. I'm glad they're on our side.

Napoleon clears his throat. "I propose the following high-level plan: Break their ranks with cannon fodder, then hit their infantry with ours, while some portion of our dreamwalkers take care of their cavalry. The rest of the dreamwalkers take to the air."

"What about him?" Felix thrusts a metal finger in Phobetor's direction.

"He expects the sisters to attack him, right?" Napoleon asks.

"Yep," I say. "Did Asha tell you about the prophecy?"

"She did," he replies. "Can you teleport over to the target?"

"That doesn't work on the battlefield," Maxwell says. "It's possible to teleport away, but then when you teleport back, it would be to the farthest edge of the field."

"So it's a lot like a normal battle," Napoleon muses. "In that case, given that he's expecting you, the last thing we want is for you to approach him head on."

"But if we don't, we can't win," Asha says, and I can tell she almost adds, "Assuming there's any way we *can* win."

"As dreamwalkers, you can change your appearances, can't you?" Napoleon asks. "For what I have in mind, I'd want the sisters not to look like themselves. Two other dreamwalkers will pretend to be them."

Asha and Kojo exchange a glance, and she morphs into him while he turns into her.

I make myself look like Valerian, and in his voice say, "We need one more me."

The Escapist woman with noble features morphs into another Asha—which is the same thing as me.

"Make your hair fiery," I say and demonstrate.

A second later, she's a dead ringer for me.

"Excellent." Napoleon gleefully rubs his small hands together. "The two decoy twins will openly go for the big target by air, while the camouflaged ones can travel on foot—as it should be easier to get lost in the sea of infantry."

"The twins shouldn't use their powers either," Asha —who's really Kojo—says. "If Phobetor doesn't realize you're dreamwalkers, the camouflage will be that much better."

Maxwell nods approvingly. "It's a much better plan than when my wife and I tried to defeat Phobetor. Maybe you will actually succeed."

"We'd better get started," Kojo—who's really Asha— says. "At any moment, someone can kill us in the real world."

As if to confirm her words, one of the Escapists poofs out of existence, and with him, a small army of dream constructs as well.

My chest tightens. "It must've been the orcs. They're still on the loose on the Escapist side of Soma."

"It's time then," Maxwell says. "Get in position."

We do our best, but due to the size of our army, this takes a while.

"Let's arm the troops," Napoleon says.

"Guns won't work," Maxwell says. "Bows and arrows might, and something like a ballista, but the most effective will be close-range weapons, like swords, axes, and machetes."

That makes sense, at least given my own experience with the subdreams.

After a quick deliberation, the dreamwalkers among us arm anyone who needs it, then manifest weapons for themselves.

I end up with a perfectly balanced katana on my back and a bow and arrow in my hands. My sister (as Kojo) manifests herself a crossbow and a sword that's a copy of the ones we use on Soma.

When all the preparations are complete, Maxwell comes over to where camouflaged Asha and I stand among the non-dreamwalkers.

"Are you sure about this?" I ask him. "You've been free all these years…"

Maxwell nods, face taut. "Farewell."

With that, his face muscles go slack, and his posture softens, as if he's removed the weight of the world from his shoulders.

The dessert-themed environment around us is replaced with that of the subdream, with the magma sky above and the black ocean below.

Like a bolt of lightning, a tendril of magma strikes Maxwell's head. Then it swirls and grows until it looks like a tornado of fire. From his eyes streams a fiery light, forming a strange hologram in the air as if the eyes were some weird movie projectors.

It's a representation of a brain, I realize, staring at the hologram in shock. His?

At first, the brain is a healthy pink, but then fire spreads through it, taking over the neurons. At the same time, an army of subdream creatures appears in the distance in front of us—a million times more frightening now that they're their usual size.

Behind them, far in the distance is Phobetor, his beautiful face both terrifying and unreadable as the fire consumes the rest of the hologram brain.

An inhuman wail escapes Maxwell's lips—and just like that, my father disappears.

CHAPTER THIRTY

"ZOMBIES, ATTACK!" Napoleon screams from his position in the back.

With a slight eyeroll, Rowan gestures at the monster horde, and her zombies charge.

There's a second of eerie silence, and then the zombies and the subdream creatures clash.

Now one can hear body parts getting ripped off, tentacles slashed, and mandibles broken—and fountains of sticky green goop and blood float on top of the black water like macabre modern art.

"Make more zombies," Napoleon orders when the first wave is all but gone—after barely destroying one percent of the enemy army.

The other dreamwalkers make more corpses, but my sister and I abstain so as not to reveal our powers.

This second group of zombies charges, but we're on the radar of the subdream monsters now.

A group of flying creatures whoosh in our

direction. They look like a hybrid between heavy-duty excavators and condors, and their shrieks make even Vickie, the siren, cringe.

Ariel aims her bow at the sky and looses an arrow.

"Anyone know what a group of condors is called?" she asks as the arrow hits one of the flying creatures in the eye.

"A condo," Felix says and launches the four giant rocks he's been holding in each of the hands of his suit.

One of the rocks bashes the condor that Ariel already wounded on the head, and the thing drops, squashing some of the enemy troops as a bonus.

The ballista fires with a loud snap, dropping a dozen condors.

Moving with uber superspeed, Ariel grabs another arrow from her quiver and downs another bird. "Is that short for condominium?"

Rowan shoots her crossbow, hitting another condor in the chest. "I actually think the term is 'scarcity.'"

Ariel looses yet another arrow, finishing the monster Rowan hit. "That's dumb. What we have is an abundance of condors, or the opposite of a scarcity."

That's an understatement. The condo or so-called scarcity of these monsters is a hundred thousand strong.

"Everyone, fire!" Napoleon shrieks.

We obey, releasing a cloud of arrows and rocks so thick it blots out the magma sky.

Most of the condors get pierced by the projectiles, but a few manage to survive.

They dive for us.

The siren shrieks upward, and two seconds later, any birds within earshot are stripped to constituent parts. Still, some are mid-dive, including one that seems to be headed for—

I swing my katana just as a beak smashes into my temple, nearly blinding me with pain as I slice the creature in half.

Staggering, I prepare to leave my body to heal myself, then remember that the plan calls for hiding my powers.

Kojo—the real one—must've been keeping an eye on the proceedings. He waves his/Asha's hand, and my wound instantly heals.

"Air support!" Napoleon yells as another condo/scarcity of flying monsters swoops our way.

A large portion of the Escapists take flight, including the fake twins. They start shooting multicolored lightning bolts at the horrific birds, lighting up the sky like fireworks.

Some condors make it through and dive down at us again.

"My zombies are gone!" Rowan yells. "Make more."

Before anyone can do that, a condor smashes into Napoleon's head, and the general disappears.

"Should I bring him back?" I urgently ask my sister. "I'm the only one who has the link."

"It's not worth revealing yourself," she replies in Kojo's voice. "Instead, help me make sure the monsters don't kill my husband."

Of course. If that happens, Kojo will turn homicidally insane—not something I want for my sister and niece.

Before I can reply, yet another condor swoops down, and I cleave it in half with my katana.

Horrific shrieks emanate from the battlefield. It's a squadron of tardigrade-like beasts; they're slithering toward us with a speed one wouldn't expect from their ten-foot-long sea-cow bodies.

Both Rowan's zombies and our dream constructs rush to intercept.

In the distance, the warthog/mole rat cavalry mobilize, so the remaining Escapists take flight and rush over there, as per Napoleon's plan.

The tardigrades slam into our forces and kill a bunch of my patients, as well as the dream construct of Napoleon, before anyone can react. Moments later, a large contingent of zombies are also torn apart by tardigrade claws, and one large monster manages to bite off Frankenstein's head.

A condor gets too close to Kojo. Moving in unison, my sister and I launch arrows at the monster, piercing it in the chest and the head.

Robin Hood avenges his fallen dream-construct comrade by turning the large tardigrade into a pincushion with his arrows, but he pays with his life when eight claws of another rip him into shreds.

In the sky, a cloud of skeletal turkey vultures comes to the aid of the condors.

Ariel takes one of them out with her bow. "I think a

group of vultures is called a kettle," she says, eyes narrowed.

Felix hurls a stone but misses his vulture. "Or a committee."

Rowan chuckles. "My favorite collective noun for vultures is a wake. Now, what do you call a group of collective nouns?"

Ariel dispatches a condor and a vulture. "Maybe a glaring of nouns, like with cats?"

Ignoring the rest of that insane conversation, I check on our Escapist air support, particularly my brother-in-law.

Though they're making decent progress with the bird menace, I can't help the feeling that their colorful lightning attacks aren't as imaginative or effective as mine would've been. Kojo is probably the most effective fighter among them—which might be why the birds attack him more often. That or the fact that he looks like Asha and is therefore on Phobetor's hit list.

I explain my observations to Asha, ending with, "I expected more from the Escapists, given their extensive experience with dreamwalking."

Kojo's eyebrows furrow on my sister's face. "Violence isn't something they've ever encountered. That's the cost of living a sheltered life."

"What about splitting into multiple selves?" I get a clear shot and down one of the vultures. "That's something they could try to speed things up."

She also shoots down a bird. "That technique is

taboo in Escapist society. I've learned how to do it, but I'm not typical."

A kettle of vultures breaks through the wall of the Escapists, and Asha and I focus on shooting them down.

When we're done, I turn my attention to the battle being waged in the distance.

The Escapists' sub-squadron smashes into the warthog/mole rat cavalry, pulverizing mount and rider alike. The battle with the tardigrades is also going well for our cannon fodder troops—that is, until the arrival of nail-swordsmen, humanoid creatures with claws as long and sharp as my katana.

Two of these newcomers rend Joygasm Troglodyte and Tarzan apart before either can so much as throw a punch.

With a sonic boom, Zorro's whip wraps around the neck of one of the nail-swordsmen. Then Zorro beheads the thing with his sword before slashing his signature Z on the defeated foe's chest. But in the process, he turns his back on one of the surviving tardigrades—and is instantly gouged by eight of the monster's claws.

Two vultures careen at my sister's husband. She and I move in sync, releasing arrows at the same time.

Two dead vultures spiral down, leaving streaks of goopy blood in their wake.

Kojo is safe for now.

Meanwhile, nearby, Zeus smites the tardigrade with

a bolt of lightning not unlike the ones the Escapists are shooting at the birds in the sky.

A nail-swordsman hurls Dream Chester at Zeus, giving another one of his kind a chance to chop both Chester and Zeus into kebabs.

Moving with vampire speed, Dracula dashes for the nail-swordsman and rips the monster's throat out with his fangs. He then tears the claws from his victim's hands and hurls them at a tardigrade nearby as if they were blades.

A thin nail-swordsman leaps into the air, beheading Dracula mid-flight—which is when Dream Itzel hurls one of her lightning ball projectiles at him, leaving behind nothing but ashes.

"Bailey's constructs kick ass," Ariel exclaims.

"You're just saying that because that version of you is the best of the bunch," Rowan says with a hint of jealousy. The construct version of her is already dead, though I have no idea how or who took her out.

And indeed, Dream Ariel moves with uber speed, slashing off mandibles and tentacles from every creature that comes her way.

Our attention must be a jinx. Dream Ariel miscalculates a leap at a nail-swordsman and gets disabled.

Itzel avenges Ariel with a lightning ball, but is then beheaded herself.

"Dream me is also doing well," Felix says. "Much better than the dream constructs the Escapists created."

Both statements are true. His robot suit is covered

in subcreature goo as Dream Felix rips other creatures into pieces. In contrast, the Escapists' creations are having their asses handed to them. Most are just copies of the Escapists themselves, but without dreamwalker powers. They're basically engaged in fisticuffs. However, they're still not as bad as their creatures from myths; those are almost comical. Case in point, the unicorn with humanoid arms—a being that a lot of them manifested. Its modus operandi is to try to tickle enemies to death, with predictable results.

Meanwhile, another vampire I made—Edith—rains havoc on the enemy forces, making me wish I'd manifested more vampire-based dream constructs. But it's too late now. I can't use my powers—especially not when condors and vultures keep swooping in, trying to kill Kojo. Two pairs of them do this now, and my sister and I are joined by Felix and Ariel as we down the monsters, then preemptively kill a few nearby vultures as well.

Spiral worms, ants, and anglers join the cannon fodder battle. Soon, the zombies are all dead—or whatever the appropriate term is—and all the Escapists are too busy with their own fighting to make more.

The Escapists in the sky are being herded back toward Phobetor, while the ones attacking the cavalry are doing a bit better. They've defeated about half their targets and are battling the rest.

It's getting harder to defend Kojo from this distance.

At least for me. Ariel looses an arrow at a condor

who's flying at the fake me—and she's farther from us than Kojo is. The arrow hits the creature's heart, slaying it instantly.

"Anyone who can fly should boost our air support!" Ariel yells.

"Smart," my sister says. "I should've given that command."

I tell her not to beat herself up; after all, Ariel is former military and my sister was almost as sheltered as the Escapists.

On Ariel's command, some of the superheroes and gods from the dream construct troops launch into the sky, as do some of the dreamers that Maxwell recruited from the Otherlands.

I was right. He's gotten to know some powerful people.

With the superheroes and gods away, the battle gets tougher for our cannon fodder.

Kit turns into a copy of Colton, and the two of them stand back to back, stomping on any monster brave or foolish enough to come at them. This goes on for a while, until two enormous condors swoop down and smash into the giant figures' heads.

The condors die on impact, but they stun Kit and Colton long enough for a colony of ant monsters to swarm them, their mandibles leaving nothing behind.

A pang of anxiety washes over me as I watch a nail-swordsman behead Dream Valerian.

Though it may not be rational to retaliate for the killing of a dream construct, I put an arrow into that nail-swordsman's eye. Watching it die is satisfying, so I figure it's good for my morale.

How is the real Valerian doing in the waking world?

No time to ponder that. The ground battle is escalating. A spiral worm leaps on Dream Felix, peeling him out of his suit so that an angler can pierce his neck with those shark-teeth.

At the same time, a tardigrade slashes the throat of the construct-siren mid-shout, just as a turkey vulture swoops in and takes out Dream Maxwell.

A whole committee of vultures somehow gets past the Escapists and swoops down. The ballista takes out four of the birds, and I join everyone in slaughtering the rest.

It's hard to keep track of the battlefield now. Superheroes and gods take the brunt of the attacks, but their ranks are thinning. The dream constructs that are most effective are duplicates of the New York Councilors and their equivalents from the other worlds. Dream Nina works closely with Fabian in wolf form and with Stanislav, who's armed with a saber. She throws half the creatures in her way onto Fabian's teeth and claws, and the rest onto Stanislav's saber.

That is, until a turkey vulture fractures the telekinetic's spine with its beak, and an angler finishes her.

Fabian leaps at the vulture, rending it with his claws. Somehow, the vulture stays alive long enough to drag the werewolf twenty feet into the air before dying

—at which point, Fabian crashes into a tardigrade and also perishes.

Thanks to his phasing, Stanislav is like a mini-army. He pierces two foes—an ant and a spiral worm—with his rapier, phases when a nail-swordsman tries to shear off the top of his head, then kills the monster with a touch.

Forget vampires, I should've manifested more chorts.

Still, the cannon fodder troops are dwindling fast. Eventually, even the likes of Stanislav can't manage the onslaught. An angler gets the chort near the end, and the rest of the monsters finish off anyone left.

"Infantry, attack!" Ariel shouts.

Pucking puck.

Infantry is us, and unlike the dream constructs, my sister and I will face dire consequences if we die.

CHAPTER THIRTY-ONE

WE SMASH into the enemy army before they can regroup from the fight with our cannon fodder troops.

The New York Councilors and their Maxwell-recruited equivalents from the Otherlands are in front, displaying a staggering assortment of powers.

In the span of mere seconds, subdream monsters are torched, ruptured from the inside, split into atoms, pulverized, exploded, imploded, torn into large and small pieces, slammed into each other, and hurled at the other side of the battlefield—all with minor losses on our side.

Occasionally, a monster breaks through, and those of us in the back ranks have to dispatch them. At first, I cut them down with my bow, but then my quiver runs empty, so I toss the bow aside and slice the monsters with my katana.

It's frustrating not to be able to use my power. Here

in the dream world, I could be more destructive than any of the Councilors.

Suddenly, I hear a strange sound from our flank.

The Escapists battling warthog/mole rat riders must've lost or given up because a significant portion of the cavalry is galloping our way.

A telekinetic slings Vickie, the siren, in front of the newcomers. With a mighty shout, she rends fifty riders apart. But then one of the surviving warthog creatures pierces her chest with its spider-like legs, and she dies.

Well, "wakes up in a cold sweat" is more accurate. Either way, she's no good to us anymore unless I manage to push her back into REM sleep, which would involve using my powers.

A woman I don't know shoots black energy at a warthog, and the thing's spidery eyes instantly go blank.

Ariel downs a mole rat rider with her last arrow. "Fighting on two fronts can be a problem."

"Make me more zombies!" Rowan shouts. "I can help."

Again, if I could use my powers, I'd do better than make more zombies. Same goes for my sister.

Yet, a fresh batch of zombies shows up in the path of the cavalry. Since we're now below our air-support Escapists, I have to assume someone up there—probably Kojo—heard Rowan's plea.

As the cavalry and the zombies face off, the rest of us carve through monsters, slowly advancing toward Phobetor.

Every inch forward thins our front lines more. If this keeps up, my sister and I will be in the thick of it by the time we cross the midpoint of the enemy forces.

My body tingles with nervous anticipation, and I squeeze the hilt of the katana harder.

The last New York Councilor dies shortly; soon after that, the final one of Maxwell's recruits is killed as well.

"This is it," Ariel says with an excitement I don't share.

Then again, her sanity isn't on the line, like mine is.

With mandibles clacking, a colony of ant monsters crashes into our ranks. A big ant lunges at me, so I cleave it in two and get sprayed with disgusting gore. It takes all my willpower not to vanish the foulness using my dreamwalking skills.

Like a war goddess, Ariel races forward, chopping mandibles left and right and cleaving insectoid bodies into pieces. Felix's four arms move like a silvery blur, his upper hands tearing off antennas while his lower hands rip off ant legs at the same time.

A lot of my patients die, some in such horrible ways that I'll have to provide them with free therapy.

There's a guttural cry to my left. A spiral worm has just sliced off Rowan's head with its knife-sharp talons. Ariel dashes toward it, but I don't see what she does because a giant tardigrade looms over Asha, ready to smother her with its bulk.

Without coordinating, she and I move in unison, slashing the thick trunk of the monster from each side.

The fragmented thing dies, but two anglers take its place.

Asha slices hers into quarters as I behead mine.

Another angler attacks me. As I dodge its tentacles, I have to remind myself that the disgusting viscera covering me is part of a dream and therefore lacks viruses and bacteria.

Shark teeth pierce my left shoulder.

Yelping in pain, I cleave off the angler's head. As it drops, a wave of nausea washes over me at the rotten-fish stench of the angler's blood and the burning agony of my wound.

A nail-swordsman rakes his claws over Asha's back. She gasps in pain, and the thing lifts another sword-like claw for a death strike. I leap forward and slice off the creature's arm before it can descend.

"Thanks," Asha pants. Then her eyes widen at something behind me.

I whirl around.

A spiral worm is corkscrewing headfirst at my chest —something or someone must've launched it, like a lance.

With a shout, Ariel jumps into its path. The thing smashes through her chest and comes out on the other side—which is when I behead it.

Ariel dies.

Gritting my teeth, I chop a nearby worm into pieces, then kill a dozen more in a haze of pain and fury.

When I slow down, I realize I've been hemorrhaging all over the place, and so has my twin.

I glance up to see why her hubby or one of the other Escapists hasn't healed us yet—just as an inhumanly beautiful voice carries across the whole battlefield, conjuring terror with each syllable it utters.

"I grow bored," Phobetor says. "Now that you're firmly within my reach, behold."

Within his reach? He must mean the invisible line through the battlefield that Maxwell drew for us earlier.

We did cross it, some time ago. There wasn't a choice. To kill him, we need to get close to him.

Phobetor waves his gargantuan hand.

Like the bolt of magma lightning that struck Maxwell, a tendril from the sky leaps into the head of the fake me— an Escapist woman whose name I didn't even learn.

The tendril then swirls and grows, until it looks like a tornado of fire. A fiery light streams from my duplicate's eyes, forming a brain hologram in the air.

Within seconds, the fire takes over the brain, and she disappears.

Phobetor's voice takes on a new inflection. "Interesting. That wasn't who I thought it was."

Another tendril careens toward the head of fake Asha, who's really Kojo.

Without losing his wife's guise, Kojo extends his hand, and even from this distance, I can see his/our features contort with strain.

The tendril meant for him shimmers in the air, then dissipates.

"Wow," I breathe. "Kojo is able to resist Phobetor."

"Perhaps at this distance," my sister whispers. "If he were closer, I doubt—"

Phobetor waves again.

All the remaining condors and vultures morph into shards of obsidian that career at the heads of Kojo and the Escapists too fast for my eyes to track.

Bam. The projectiles bash against all the heads as one, leaving the stunned dreamwalkers floating in the air.

Suddenly, every molecule in my body feels heavy, as if gravity has quadrupled. And that must be exactly what's happened. Blood gushes faster from my shoulder, and it's a struggle to remain on my feet.

Kojo plummets from the sky, along with the other Escapists.

Puck. If they hit the ground, their minds will be broken beyond repair.

"No!" Asha yells and extends her hand toward her husband.

There's a blur of movement in my periphery.

I twist for it, sword ready—but it's too late.

The moment of distraction has given a nail-swordsman an opportunity, and the beast has cashed it by burying its sword-like claws in my sister's stomach.

CHAPTER THIRTY-TWO

AS I BEHEAD my sister's attacker, I make the fastest decision of my life.

If I don't use my powers, Asha and her husband will end up homicidally insane, as will their fellow Escapists.

No. Not on my watch.

Feeling like I'm throwing off shackles, I summon my dreamwalking ability and heal Asha's wound. Then I counter Phobetor's gravity reversal with one of my own, adding in extra air resistance for good measure.

Kojo's lethal plummet slows to the gentle downward drift of a feather.

I start to jolt him awake, but another tendril leaps out of the magma sky and strikes his head. Again, a brain hologram shows up, and as I watch in horror, my brother-in-law is Overtaken.

Then this happens to another Escapist.

And another.

I shake off my stunned paralysis and channel all of my terror and grief into jolting the rest of the Escapists awake.

To my shock, it works, though this is exponentially more people than the maximum I've jolted before.

Asha must realize our power embargo is at an end because my shoulder heals, as do the other aches and pains in my body.

Phobetor gestures again.

Felix's suit melts around him until nothing is left as every single one of our remaining allies dies in similarly torturous ways—and no matter how much I push back with my power, I'm unable to stop the slaughter.

Soon, Asha and I are the only ones left, and our disguises disappear, leaving us looking like twins again.

Staring at the monsters around us with anguished eyes, Asha jerkily makes a circle with her hand.

The nearby monsters turn into vapor mid-leap.

I do the same, trying to ignore the fear squeezing my chest, the awful certainty that we are losing.

"We need to keep fighting," I tell Asha when her gaze meets mine, but I can see the same despair written on her face.

Still, her back straightens, and she nods grimly.

We turn to attack a new crop of monsters, but we don't get far.

Two new bolts of magma snake from the sky toward us.

Asha extends her hand, her features contorting in an echo of Kojo's strained expression.

The fiery tendrils shimmer in the air and dissipate.

Two more show up, and Asha destroys them too.

In the distance, Phobetor's figure grows impossibly larger. "End them!" his terrifyingly beautiful voice booms, and millions of his minions close ranks around us, like a hangman's noose.

CHAPTER THIRTY-THREE

"MULTIBODY TECHNIQUE!" I shout as I leave my body.

Leveraging my panic and desperation, I make two of me, then the two make four, and those four make eight, and so on until my powers fail on the twentieth split—but by then, there are more than a million me, for such is the power of exponential growth.

Asha has done the same, but faster and one extra time, so there are over two million versions of her on the battlefield now.

Each of us is hungry for battle.

The only problem with splitting so many times is that it leaves very little power to do anything flashy to the monsters. No matter. We kill them with our katanas, while Ashas do the same with their swords.

One of me kills a vulture and an angler in a single strike.

Nearby, a version of my sister beheads a tardigrade and disembowels a nail-swordsman.

"How about you and I act as generals from my dream palace?" I pant. "I think the rest of us won't miss us."

She nods, and I use what little power I have left to teleport the two of us into that very familiar environment as the legions of ourselves continue cutting through the monsters toward Phobetor.

Once inside the dream palace, I face her. "What's the new plan?"

In the time I ask the question, hundreds more monsters are slain by us on the battlefield.

"I don't know." Asha looks hunted. "Maybe we figure out the Two as One thing?"

"Even if we do, then what?"

She chews on her bottom lip. "The copies of us could hold back the subdream monsters as we approach Phobetor and use the mystery skill to kill him."

As she speaks, the other us advance toward our enemy.

Worryingly, Phobetor doesn't look at all intimidated.

"We're overleveraged on dreamwalker powers," I say. "I could barely teleport the two of us here."

Asha squares her shoulders. "Let's think positive. Maybe the mystery technique needs only a little power. If so, I could spare that."

"Fine. Let's focus on figuring out the Two as One bit." I rake my fingers through my fiery hair. "The stress isn't helping jog my memory at all."

Asha nods grimly. "I'm drawing a blank too—exactly as if there were a black window blocking my childhood from me. Except I could never locate one, same as you."

Even though I know it's pointless, I look around.

Nope.

No black windows have magically materialized.

Feeling silly, I even look up.

Nope.

Just the usual decorative mosaic depicting an archery-target-like mandala made out of multicolored glass.

My stomach drops.

Glass.

Multicolored.

"It can't be," I mutter.

Uncomprehending, my sister follows my gaze.

I jab my finger at the mosaic. "The bullseye. There, in the very center. It's the darkest piece. Isn't it black?"

"It is," she breathes, awed.

"Isn't a window a piece of glass?" I press on. "Maybe they're usually bigger, and on walls, but—"

Asha extends a trembling hand, a glimmer of hope returning to her eyes. "I might have enough juice to take you through it."

I clasp her hand, and she rockets up.

As the bullseye nears, I realize that it isn't even all that much smaller than a window. Being a piece in a mosaic makes it appear that way, especially from the very bottom of the lobby.

It has to be the black window we've missed all these years—we just didn't see it as such because we've grown to see the mosaic as a whole, not a sum of its parts.

It must be what's hiding our childhood memories.

It's our only chance.

Sure enough, as soon as the top of Asha's head touches the bullseye, the dream palace around us evaporates.

———

WE'RE in a room covered from floor to ceiling with pottery paraphernalia, everything from wheel to kiln.

"We made it," Asha exclaims, looking around in wonder. "For a moment there, I thought I was going to drown in that black water, towing you along."

That's right. This time, I was the unconscious one inside the boat. "This is my first time experiencing this from this end," I say. "What should I—"

I don't finish the sentence because memories flood in, just as this particular one starts playing in front of our eyes.

Bebe is molding a vase on the wheel.

Seeing her unlocks a cascade of recollections: her lovingly calling me "her little bee," the countless hugs she gave me, the priceless wisdom she imparted, the stories she told to lull me and Asha to sleep…

It's almost unbearable, and the tears that I couldn't shed for her earlier begin streaking down my cheeks.

But they're not just tears of sadness. Though I lost Bebe today, I've just regained a part of her as well.

A part that I will now carry in my memories.

Asha's eyes are also on Bebe, her cheeks as wet as mine.

The memory continues to play out.

Mom is sitting there with a serene expression on her face.

Seeing her triggers its own rollercoaster of childhood memories, each more treasured than the next.

The countless times she tucked me into bed.

The way she'd make the boring Soma food seem fun.

The love and warmth she'd given me.

Next to me, Asha drags in a shaky breath.

Mom is holding the young versions of us.

The recollections of my sister at that age flow in, and I feel like my mind might burst from it all.

Focusing, I strain to catch one particular memory among them—of the Two as One game—but it's too hard. Things are too jumbled at the moment.

"Come, dear ones," Bebe says in the memory.

As the two little girls shuffle over to her, I realize I've seen this very memory in Mom's black window. Except now I remember it in every detail, down to how it felt, and it's so much more vivid than when I was an observer.

"You can touch," Bebe tells the girls.

Grinning mischievously, the twins leave palmprints on the sides of the vase.

Bebe smiles in approval and deposits the vase into the kiln.

"Isn't that the vase from your memory gallery?" grown Asha asks. "The one you broke years later, on Gomorrah?"

Before I can reply in the affirmative, Bebe gives the vase to Mom as a gift, and the memory terminates.

———

THE NEW MEMORY RUNS FASTER.

We're in a different room, and I recall that it's the living room of our Soma dwelling.

I've seen this room in memories of others.

It's where Asha and I were born.

"Did anything about Two as One come back to you?" grown Asha asks.

"No." I greedily scan the room in the hopes that something here will trigger the memory we seek.

Mom is holding Dad's hand, and seeing him opens a new tsunami of recollections.

The piggyback rides.

The itchiness of his stubble when he'd kiss my cheek.

The loving way he'd gaze at us.

The feeling of safety in his embrace.

I can only think of him as Dad from now on, not

father—and certainly not something as impersonal as Maxwell.

The memory continues.

Six-year-old versions of me and Asha are playing with Valerian and Kojo while our parents converse about the prophecy.

Valerian pulls on his father's sleeve. "Dad, can Bailey and I go to the garden?"

Davu nods, and little me and little Valerian race out of the room.

Again, I can't help but remember more than the content of the memory provided.

Valerian and I were best friends, inseparable companions. He was also my first crush—and at the ripe old age of six, I made a vow to myself that I would marry him one day. There was even a chaste kiss once —our true first kiss, as it turns out.

The sweet memories stoke my fears about Valerian fighting the Overtaken in the waking world. With effort, I shake it off. I have to believe he can handle himself—and that Asha and I will be able to defeat Phobetor in time.

Young Valerian chases the young me all the way to the garden.

Asha and Kojo soon show up as well, and we play a Soma version of tag until the memory terminates.

———

THIS IS IT.

In this sped-up memory, Asha and I are in the dream world, in her childhood version of the memory gallery.

"Two as one, remember?" young me says to Asha with a small pout. "You and Kojo ran away for a whole hour. I want to know what happened."

I remember what's about to happen, and stagger as if from a blow. "We're so pucked," I say in horror as everything to do with the game clicks back into place.

Young Asha creates a painting so that the young me can leap into it.

"This is all there is to that game," I say to the wide-eyed grown Asha. "We made a pact to share every single breath with each other, so when circumstances tore us apart for a few minutes, we'd create the memory of what the other missed." As I say the words, dozens of super-cute memories of Asha's experience paintings replay in front of my mind: her playing doctor with Kojo, her getting a stubbed toe healed in the medical bay, and on and on.

Grown Asha's face blanches. "How can this help us with Phobetor?"

"It can't." I look at her mournfully. "This *is* the game our family heard about—and it has nothing at all to do with the god of nightmares."

CHAPTER THIRTY-FOUR

ASHA'S EYES ARE ENORMOUS. "But the prophecy—"

"Must be about someone else. Or 'Two as One' means something else that we didn't discover."

The memory of the game terminates, and the ones that follow are too fast to register. I don't need them, though. I remember everything. In a way, locking away my childhood preserved the memories for me. Usually, people remember only bits and pieces of theirs, but I recall it all. It just doesn't help with our predicament.

Still, if we survive, I intend to enjoy savoring each memory, finding a place for them in my palace. Then again, surviving is a big if—

———

ASHA and I are back in my dream palace lobby.

The bullseye in the middle of the target in the ceiling is no longer black.

"Should I unlock yours?" I gesture up.

"Later," she says. "After we make sure there *is* a later."

"Smart. Do you have any semblance of a plan?"

She begins to pace. "Some of our selves have reached Phobetor. Why don't we have those selves become singletons once again? This way, we'll be near him, and with our powers intact."

"But the monsters will tear us to shreds," I say.

"We'll recreate our constructs and have them protect us. Hopefully they'll last long enough for us to do the next part."

I arch an eyebrow. "And that is?"

"We attempt to become a single being again," she says in a matter-of-fact tone. "That has to be what the prophecy was about."

"You mean that technique we tried during the training? We failed at it, remember?"

"We're more motivated now," she says grimly. "And have more emotions we can channel into it as well."

That last bit is true. If emotions were electricity, I could power a small town with mine.

"Hold on," I say. "The last time we tried that trick, we got insanely tired."

"I know." She scrubs a hand over her face. "It could be our last move. Do you have a better idea?"

I shake my head.

"Then let's do it. Remember, start with the molecule trick you used to grow big, then tell your molecules to mix with mine as we hug."

"Got it," I say and teleport back to the battlefield.

———

ASHA JOINS ME IN A SECOND.

As Dad had warned us, teleporting back here puts us at the edge farthest from Phobetor.

But that is only true for these versions of us.

In the far distance, millions of others are much closer to the looming target, and two of us are exactly where they need to be.

"Time to make some of ourselves disappear," Asha says and poofs out of existence next to me.

This version of me does the same thing, as does one that's just finished killing an extra-large tardigrade. Same for a nearby me who's just beheaded a nail-swordsman.

Millions of poofs later, only one of me and Asha remain—the ones closest to Phobetor.

My full dream power is coursing through me now, no longer used up by the multibody technique.

"We need to stall the creatures," my sister shouts. "Quick!"

The creatures in question turn our way and prepare to attack en masse.

Channeling the pleasant emotions from the memories I've just recovered, I recreate every single one of my dream constructs in one giant use of power, bringing back both fictional characters and people I know in real life.

Asha does the same—but even with her additions, there aren't enough allies, not by a long shot.

"I got this." I channel my strongest emotion—anxiety over Valerian's fate—into pushing everyone I know back into REM sleep.

By all rights, this shouldn't work. I've just learned this skill, and I've only been able to do this to one person, not hundreds.

Yet it happens.

Felix, Rowan, Ariel, Napoleon, the siren, and the rest of the New York Council reappear in the path of the subdream abominations—and recover their wits quickly enough to attack.

This might buy us a little time.

"Now or never," Asha says, echoing my thoughts.

Dropping our weapons, we hug.

I close my eyes and visualize myself made from molecules. Then I will them into becoming a single person with Asha.

"How touching," Phobetor's booming voice intrudes, but I banish it from my mind, instead visualizing our molecules intermixing. "A hug and a chance to see your friends for the last time," he continues mockingly. "What's next, the last meal?"

I channel all my emotions into the desperate merging attempt.

Nothing happens at first.

Then I feel a familiar wooziness.

Asha's arms are no longer around me.

I open my eyes—or, hopefully, our eyes.

Nope.

Asha is still separate from me. She's just stepped away to dry-heave, like the last time we tried this.

I also feel sick, but I hold it in as a wave of exhaustion smashes into me.

"This is as far as your parents got," Phobetor says, and I have to crane my neck to see the malevolent expression on his ethereal face far above me. "You know what happened after that."

As a macabre underscore to his words, Rowan and Napoleon get disemboweled by the nail-swordsmen.

I glare up at the god of nightmares. "Shut the puck up. I have a promise to keep."

He scoffs. "This is your last chance to become my servants willingly." His voice evokes all my fears, like it did when I faced him in Mom's dreams. "Kneel."

Like that time, my whole being demands that I give in—only this temptation is exponentially worse. In his embrace, there will be solace. Our whole family will reunite. I'll no longer feel this overwhelming exhaustion. I'll—

"No!" both Asha and I exclaim at the same time.

I channel my wrath into my power, and just like that, I throw off his vileness and feel like myself again —except completely drained and on the verge of a panic attack.

Judging by my sister's angry glare, she's also thrown off his attempt.

"So be it." Phobetor advances toward us, hand outstretched.

Two massive bolts of magma snake down toward our heads.

Asha lifts her hand, her features contorting again, and I mirror her gesture, though I have no idea what I'm doing.

I focus on the tendril that's coming my way, willing it out of existence with all my might.

The fiery tendril shimmers in the air and dissipates.

Only mine, though.

The second one smashes into Asha's head and swirls, growing to tornado proportions until my sister's eyes begin to stream a fiery light that forms a brain hologram in the air.

No. Please no.

I strain my power to sever the horrible link for her —but to no avail.

All the parts of Asha's brain are taken over by the fire, and a pained cry escapes her lips as she disappears.

I stare at the empty spot uncomprehendingly.

On some level, I must've believed the cursed prophecy.

I thought—or hoped—that the two of us were somehow *destined* to win.

Meaning we'd find a way, against all odds.

My heart feels like it's imploding as I lift my gaze to meet Phobetor's black-hole eyes.

The prophecy was a pleasant fantasy.

Now it's just me, alone with the god of nightmares.

In a moment, he will kill or Overtake me—and that'll be the end.

CHAPTER THIRTY-FIVE

PUCK THAT.

I'm not letting that happen before I at least smack the bastard in the face.

I visualize myself as made out of molecules again, then will them to grow, channeling everything into this last-ditch attempt: the weariness, the agony of defeat, the desire to save Valerian and my family, the grief over Bebe's demise.

To my shock, I grow to Phobetor's size in an instant.

Here we go.

Balling my hands into fists, I lumber toward him.

"Nice try." He gestures at me.

This time, the fiery strand isn't a bolt but a twister. Swirling like a tornado of fire, it leaps for my giant head.

I extend my own ginormous hand and will the strand out of existence.

It reaches me anyway.

A searing pain smashes into my nerve endings.

Whatever I did to thwart this attack before clearly didn't happen this time. Unless... I didn't do anything, and it was Asha.

She protected me instead of herself.

That's why Phobetor was able to Overtake her.

Too bad her sacrifice was in vain.

Fire streams out of my eyes and forms an epic hologram of my jumbo brain behind Phobetor.

It looks odd, different than the others—and not just because of the size.

There's a network of vein-like tentacles inside my brain. *Furry* tentacles.

I try to lift my arm and find it paralyzed.

I will myself to shrink, but that doesn't work either.

The fire spreads through my holographic brain's neurons—but this, too, doesn't go as it did for everyone else.

Whenever the fire meets the furry parts of my brain, it fails to take them over.

I blink at the image, and suddenly everything slides into place.

Of course.

"Two as One" didn't refer to me and Asha. It was about me and someone else.

Someone who is closer to me than any sibling.

Someone with whom I share all my nutrients.

Someone who feels my emotions.

Someone who's always there for me in the dream world.

Someone who shares my brain—and is thus the obstacle Phobetor's power has just encountered.

Pom and I live as a single symbiotic organism.

We're Two as One.

Pom! I mentally shout. *I need you. Please be brave. I know you can do this.*

In the hologram, the furry tentacles turn from black to teal and begin pushing the fire back, clearing the other portions of the brain.

I regain the feeling in my arm, but I remain still, not letting Phobetor see it.

Let's end this, I shout inside my head.

Like we've practiced. Pom's voice is filled with determination.

What?

Phobetor's eyes narrow. He's realizing something is wrong.

A furry bracelet appears on my wrist, and I understand what Pom means.

We've trained together to defeat the monsters in the subdreams.

He's been my weapon all along.

He elongates into a furry katana, one proportional to my enormous size.

My enemy is finally within my reach.

With all my might, I slice with my furry weapon—and in the black pools of Phobetor's enormous eyes, I see both horror and surprise.

My blade bites into his neck, cutting through skin, muscle, and veins, severing cartilage and spinal cord.

As it comes out on the other side, the pull of his hypnotic stare disappears, and his head separates from his giant body, rolling over to my feet.

"I keep my promises." Vehemently, I kick the ginormous head in the face, launching it in the air like a soccer ball. "That's for my grandmother."

I feel it then.

I feel the being that was Phobetor evaporate out of existence—and as he does, a shockwave of power is unleashed.

Like a nuclear blast, it crashes into me, and everything goes totally dark.

CHAPTER THIRTY-SIX

I COME TO.

I'm alive. Yay. It would've sucked to have killed Phobetor but paid for it with my life—like a true hero of legendary prophecy.

There's a tiny, warm hand on my wrist.

I open my eyes.

I'm in the medical bay, with Chloe, my niece, at my bedside.

Seeing me awake, she springs to her feet.

"You're finally up!" she shouts with childish exuberance. "Stay there, I'm going to get someone."

"Wait, is your mommy—"

She's already gone.

Questions swirl through my groggy brain.

Where is everyone? How long was I out? Is Valerian alive? Is Dad still Overtaken? Is Asha? Is everyone else?

I push up to a sitting position and look around.

The gurneys that we were strapped to earlier are now empty—a good sign.

Mom is still here, but someone moved her onto a bed.

My heart leaps. With Phobetor gone, I can finally go into her dreams and try to get her out—but I'm going to wait for some answers before I attempt it.

My gaze falls on my furry bracelet.

Wait, Pom. That's who I need to check on first. He was there when the blast of power knocked me out, so he could've also gotten hurt.

A touch and a moment of concentration later, I'm in my dream palace once more.

Pom is here, grinning at me, his fur a deep purple.

"You're okay." I grab him in a hug and squeeze for all I'm worth.

He grunts comically, so I put him down.

He floats up to be eye-level with me. "Never been better. How about you?"

"I'm fine. Just clueless about the others."

Speaking of the others, what happened to Felix, Ariel, and the other people who kept me safe from subdream monsters?

I take Pom to the tower of sleepers to find out.

Felix and Ariel are asleep, as are the members of the New York Council.

I check on Ariel first. She tells me she's great, and that the whole thing was actually fun. I make a mental note to reject any future invitations to do something "fun" with her.

Felix is also okay, and a lot more healthily unenthusiastic about the violence he lived through. Same with everyone else I check on.

When I exit the siren's dreams, I spot a person in the tower of sleepers that I haven't seen here for a long time—not since the beginning of all my misadventures, back when she was Ariel and Felix's roommate.

Is it a coincidence that she's here now that I've thwarted an apocalypse?

No way. Given everything I know about this one, she's dreaming at just the right moment so we can chat.

Pom points at her. "Isn't that Princess Peach? Haven't seen her in forever."

Nodding, I approach the pale-skinned, black-haired woman and touch her forehead, leaping into her dreams.

———

AS I TAKE in the dream, I do a double take.

We're in my dream palace lobby.

How does she know what it looks like? I don't usually take people there.

She's standing in front of a dream version of me, who's saying, "Fine, let's talk here." And the mind-boggling part is that this dream feels like a memory.

Except I never said those words to her. Unless...

Of course. This is a seer vision of a conversation we'll have at some point in the future. Probably the very conversation I came here to have.

I dismiss the other me and change the environment to that of a desert, mainly to be contrary.

"Hey," I say. "Were you expecting me?"

A deck of cards appears in her hands as if by magic, and she gives them a practiced shuffle. "Come on. You know where this conversation is supposed to take place."

With a sigh, I take us back to my palace.

She grins. "You also know your next line."

"Fine," I say with an eye roll. "Let's talk here."

The cards disappear from her hands, again as if by magic. "I wanted to thank you and Pom for a job well done. Phobetor was a threat to my family's future—everybody's future, really—so I'm pleased he's gone."

Pom perches on my shoulder. "I'm confused. If you didn't like him, why didn't you help us?"

"Nostradamus was on it," she says with a shrug. "When that guy has a plan, it's better to stay out. I know this from personal experience. Besides, I couldn't just tell you the future. If I did, it wouldn't happen." She examines her nails. "Also, I promised my hubby not to get myself embroiled in any shenanigans—particularly of an apocalyptic type—for at least a few centuries. He would've been growly if I'd lied."

A strong headache begins to thud in my temples, so I quickly jump out of my body to cure it.

I think if I talked to seers more often, I'd lose my pucking mind.

"You're welcome," Pom says in the meanwhile.

I sigh again. "Was there anything else?" I ask her. "I need to wake up to check on more people."

"Here's a little gift," she says. "The people you want to check on are all fine, and most of your possible futures are long and happy, especially for you and your husband." She makes an oops face. "I meant, your boyfriend. No, wait, is it too soon even for that? Your hookup?"

Pom's eyes widen. "Is she serious?"

I don't answer because my headache is returning again. My mind reels. As a seer, she knows what the future brings, but she's also a mischievous jokester, so how can I know if she's telling the truth? Especially that bit about Valerian and me getting married? By telling me this information, she may well be starting a chain of events that leads me to do her a favor in a "few centuries," when her "hubby" lets her get back to "shenanigans."

"They're waiting," she says with a smirk. "I feel like I've done my part."

With that, she wakes up.

Exchanging an exasperated glance with Pom, I return to the real world.

———

"I'M TELLING YOU, she was up," my niece is saying.

I open my eyes again.

Besides Chloe, surrounding my bed are Dad, Valerian, Kojo, and Asha.

My chest feels warm and tingly.

"You're okay, right?" Chloe asks. "Say yes."

"Yes," I say, smiling at her. I look around. "What about all of you?"

Valerian nods, his eyes gleaming brightly. "As soon as you won, the Overtaken became themselves once again. I had the good fortune to last until then."

I leap off the bed and tackle-hug him. Then I hug everyone else.

Pom's fur is the deepest, happiest purple I've ever seen.

Though the seer had just told me they're fine, I had to see it with my own eyes, feel them with my own hands.

Not for a second does my worry about germs kick in with all this touching. It was like that with Mom, my only other family until now, so I guess it makes sense.

My heart expands at the thought.

I have so much family!

"How long was I out?" I ask, trying to contain my excitement.

"Almost a day." Valerian frowns. "Got me worried."

"I got *you* worried?" I exclaim. "I wasn't the one fighting an army of the Overtaken."

"No one has been able to do what you did," Dad says. "We didn't know what to expect."

"Right," I say. "So what happened while I was out?"

Valerian clasps my hand with both of his, his palms big and warm around my fingers. "The newly freed

Overtaken helped us with the wounded and the dead. The necromancer was especially useful."

Asha looks at our joined hands and gives me a surreptitious wink. "Afterward, we escorted them all far away from Soma and locked away their memories of it."

"That's a busy day." I glance at Mom's unconscious body. "What about her?"

Dad follows my gaze. "I waited for you, so I could ask for a favor."

I look at him.

"I know you've worked really hard to bring her out of that comatose state—and I'll be forever grateful to you for that. But I was wondering if you'd let me do this last part. She might be more receptive if—"

"Of course." I actually feel a little relieved. A part of me was dreading trying this again—and possibly failing. "I just want to get her back."

"I'll do it now," Dad says solemnly. "And I'll make sure she's got all her memories back while I'm at it."

I face Asha. "Speaking of memories… Did you—"

"Yes," my sister says. "I remember you now. As soon as there was a quiet moment, Kojo unlocked the black window for me. I now remember you, Dad, Mom, and Valerian."

My eyes sweep over everyone in the room. "I also got it all back," I say softly. I meet Valerian's gaze. "And I mean, *everything*."

His ocean-blue eyes are warm and bright, like tropical waters. Suddenly, the medical bay morphs into

Valerian's living room—and the illusion makes it so we're the only ones there.

"You're giving us privacy?" On my wrist, Pom's fur turns coral pink.

He nods, squeezing my hand tighter. "Before the Overtaken attacked, you wanted to talk," he murmurs. "What about?"

"Ah, that." I give him a mischievous grin. All my uncertainty about us is gone. "I think I've figured it all out. Memories of us as kids really helped."

He arches an eyebrow. "Care to include me in your revelations?"

"If I must." My grin widens. "I know you're crazy about me. I'm beginning to warm up to you also. What do you say we see where that leads us?"

I decide not to tell him about the seer's "husband" prognostication. She said knowing the future could change it, so why tempt fate?

A slow, dangerously sexy smile curves his lips. "Are you saying you want to go steady?"

In answer, I rise up on tiptoes and kiss him. There are no thoughts of germs in my mind, no thoughts of anything but the man in front of me and the heat streaking down my spine as his skilled tongue dances with mine for several long moments.

Reluctantly, he pulls away, and the illusion disappears, revealing the medical bay and the rest of my family.

"Now we just need to get her back," Dad is saying as he strides over to Mom's bed.

My breath catches, and I forget all about the kiss.

This is it.

Valerian squeezes my hand reassuringly as Dad touches Mom's forehead with his fingertips and closes his eyes.

We all wait in tense silence.

The seconds tick on.

My eyes meet Asha's, and I can see the same worry on her face.

What if it fails?

What if the accident did some irreversible damage after all?

Even Chloe is still, a tiny V between her little brows. She can sense the somber mood of the adults.

Dad removes his hand from Mom's forehead.

I can't see his face, so I have no idea if he's triumphant or devastated.

Slowly, I start toward the bed—and as I'm reaching out to touch Mom's hand, she smiles and opens her eyes.

EPILOGUE

EVERYONE WHO PARTICIPATED in the battle against Phobetor is in the dream world with all of Soma, my new home.

Over the last few weeks, my sister and I have convinced both sides of Soma, the Escapists and the others, to reunite into one people, and now all of us have gathered to honor the ones who perished during The Attack—including Soma's fallen leader, my grandmother and namesake, Bailey.

Soma funerals have two parts, Body and Mind. The Body part happens in the real world, where the flesh of the departed is recycled by special machines that perpetuate the cycle of life in the colony. The Mind portion happens in the dream world, like many other Soman rites of passage. Here, a dream construct of the departed is created jointly by everyone their life had touched, and then the construct delivers a farewell speech—a kind of reverse eulogy.

"Dear citizens of Soma," Bebe's construct says from a large podium. "During this somber occasion, I beg you to be joyful." Smiling beatifically, she looks at where our family is sitting. "The goal that our people have been toiling toward for countless generations has now been achieved. Nightmares are back to being mere dreams and no longer threaten to tear families apart. You get to return to normal—whatever will pass for normal in the future, be it parking this colony ship on a planet, or taking it on an interstellar voyage, or something I can't even imagine, being gone and all." She locks eyes with me. "Be at ease. I would gladly give up my life many times over for what we have accomplished. For the new world we created." She turns her gaze to my niece. "A world where my great-granddaughter can thrive. A world where..."

I miss the rest as Mom, who's standing next to me, begins crying—only to be embraced by Dad. She's been crying a lot since she woke up, tears both of pain and joy. Pain for all the years our family's been torn apart, for all the guilt and shame she'd carried in her subconscious for so long... for the desperation that drove her to throw herself under that car, and for everything that followed. Today, though, her tears are for her mother, and all the other people she's just recently remembered, only to discover they'd died during The Attack.

My own throat feels thick and swollen, my face wet. But underneath the pain of loss is hope. Hope that the future will be brighter than the past, that everything my family has been through has only made us stronger. And sure enough, as Bebe's eulogy proceeds, Mom lifts her face from Dad's shoulder and gives me a smile so full of tenderness and joy that I can't help but smile back and reach for her.

My twin, her thoughts mirroring mine, as they often do, steps up at the same time, and we all hug— Mom, Dad, and the two of us—treasuring this moment.

When I finally draw back, it's into the supportive arms of Valerian, who lends me his strength as the eulogy concludes.

I look up at him, and as our eyes meet, I know that with him and my family by my side, I can get through anything... even defeat another god.

As the Mind ceremony comes to an end, the fireworks begin—pyrotechnics that involve big bangs that birth baby universes like colorful bubbles in the sky above us.

It's the most majestic display the dreamwalkers of Soma could conjure up to honor the ones we lost—and a fitting farewell.

SNEAK PEEKS

Thank you for reading! I hope you enjoyed Bailey's story.

Do you want to be notified of my new releases? Sign up for my email list at www.dimazales.com!

Love audiobooks? This series, and all of my other books, are available in audio.

Want to read my other books? You can check out:

- *The Sasha Urban Series* - the fantastical urban fantasy series set in the same universe as Bailey Spade, where Felix and Ariel first appear
- *Mind Dimensions* - the action-packed urban fantasy adventures of Darren, who can stop time and read minds

- *Upgrade* - the thrilling sci-fi tale of Mike Cohen, whose new technology will transform our brains *and* the world
- *The Last Humans* - the futuristic sci-fi/dystopian story of Theo, who lives in a world where nothing is as it seems
- *The Sorcery Code* - the epic fantasy adventures of sorcerer Blaise and his creation, the beautiful and powerful Gala

And now, please turn the page for a sneak peek at *The Sorcery Code.*

SNEAK PEEK AT THE SORCERY CODE

Once a respected member of the Sorcerer Council and now an outcast, Blaise has spent the last year of his life working on a special magical object. The goal is to allow anyone to do magic, not just the sorcerer elite. The outcome of his quest is unlike anything he could've ever imagined—because, instead of an object, he creates Her.

She is Gala, and she is anything but inanimate. Born in the Spell Realm, she is beautiful and highly intelligent —and nobody knows what she's capable of. She will do anything to experience the world... even leave the man she is beginning to fall for.

Augusta, a powerful sorceress and Blaise's former fiancée, sees Blaise's deed as the ultimate hubris and Gala as an abomination that must be destroyed. In her quest to save the human race, Augusta will forge new alliances, becoming tangled in a web of intrigue that stretches further than any of them suspect. She may even have to turn to her new lover Barson, a ruthless warrior who might have an agenda of his own...

————

There was a naked woman on the floor of Blaise's study.

A beautiful naked woman.

Stunned, Blaise stared at the gorgeous creature who just appeared out of thin air. She was looking around with a bewildered expression on her face, apparently as shocked to be there as he was to be seeing her. Her wavy blond hair streamed down her back, partially covering a body that appeared to be perfection itself. Blaise tried not to think about that body and to focus on the situation instead.

A woman. A *She*, not an *It*. Blaise could hardly believe it. Could it be? Could this girl be the object?

She was sitting with her legs folded underneath her, propping herself up with one slim arm. There was something awkward about that pose, as though she didn't know what to do with her own limbs. In general, despite the curves that marked her a fully grown woman, there was a child-like innocence in the way she sat there, completely unselfconscious and totally unaware of her own appeal.

Clearing his throat, Blaise tried to think of what to say. In his wildest dreams, he couldn't have imagined this kind of outcome to the project that had consumed his entire life for the past several months.

Hearing the sound, she turned her head to look at him, and Blaise found himself staring into a pair of unusually clear blue eyes.

She blinked, then cocked her head to the side, studying him with visible curiosity. Blaise wondered what she was seeing. He hadn't seen the light of day in weeks, and he wouldn't be surprised if he looked like a mad sorcerer at this point. There was probably a week's worth of stubble covering his face, and he knew his dark hair was unbrushed and sticking out in every direction. If he'd known he would be facing a beautiful woman today, he would've done a grooming spell in the morning.

"Who am I?" she asked, startling Blaise. Her voice was soft and feminine, as alluring as the rest of her. "What is this place?"

"You don't know?" Blaise was glad he finally managed to string together a semi-coherent sentence. "You don't know who you are or where you are?"

She shook her head. "No."

Blaise swallowed. "I see."

"What am I?" she asked again, staring at him with those incredible eyes.

"Well," Blaise said slowly, "if you're not some cruel prankster or a figment of my imagination, then it's somewhat difficult to explain..."

She was watching his mouth as he spoke, and when he stopped, she looked up again, meeting his gaze. "It's strange," she said, "hearing words this way. These are the first real words I've heard."

Blaise felt a chill go down his spine. Getting up from his chair, he began to pace, trying to keep his eyes off her nude body. He had been expecting something to appear. A magical object, a thing. He just hadn't known what form that thing would take. A mirror, perhaps, or a lamp. Maybe even something as unusual as the Life Capture Sphere that sat on his desk like a large round diamond.

But a person? A female person at that?

To be fair, he had been trying to make the object intelligent, to ensure it would have the ability to comprehend human language and convert it into the code. Maybe he shouldn't be so surprised that the intelligence he invoked took on a human shape.

A beautiful, feminine, sensual shape.

Focus, Blaise, focus.

"Why are you walking like that?" She slowly got to her feet, her movements uncertain and strangely clumsy. "Should I be walking too? Is that how people talk to each other?"

Blaise stopped in front of her, doing his best to keep his eyes above her neck. "I'm sorry. I'm not accustomed to naked women in my study."

She ran her hands down her body, as though trying to feel it for the first time. Whatever her intent, Blaise found the gesture extremely erotic.

"Is something wrong with the way I look?" she

asked. It was such a typical feminine concern that Blaise had to stifle a smile.

"Quite the opposite," he assured her. "You look unimaginably good." So good, in fact, that he was having trouble concentrating on anything but her delicate curves. She was of medium height, and so perfectly proportioned that she could've been used as a sculptor's template.

"Why do I look this way?" A small frown creased her smooth forehead. "What am I?" That last part seemed to be puzzling her the most.

Blaise took a deep breath, trying to calm his racing pulse. "I think I can try to venture a guess, but before I do, I want to give you some clothing. Please wait here —I'll be right back."

And without waiting for her answer, he hurried out of the room.

————

Visit www.dimazales.com to learn more!

ABOUT THE AUTHOR

Dima Zales is a *New York Times* and *USA Today* bestselling author of science fiction and fantasy. Prior to becoming a writer, he worked in the software development industry in New York as both a programmer and an executive. From high-frequency trading software for big banks to mobile apps for popular magazines, Dima has done it all. In 2013, he left the software industry in order to concentrate on his writing career and moved to Palm Coast, Florida, where he currently resides.

Please visit www.dimazales.com to learn more.